I Stole You

stories from the fae

I Stole You

stories from the fae

Kristen Ringman

Handtype Press
Minneapolis, MN

Stories

Where the wave of moonlight glosses
The dim gray sands with light,
Far off by furthest Rosses
We foot it all the night,
Weaving olden dances
Mingling hands and mingling glances
Till the moon has taken flight;
To and fro we leap
And chase the frothy bubbles,
While the world is full of troubles
And anxious in its sleep.
Come away, O human child!
To the waters and the wild
With a faery, hand in hand,
For the world's more full of weeping than
    you can understand.

— *W. B. Yeats*

for Willow,
you stole me from 2002 until 2012

I'd like to think I've stolen you forever

The Meaning, Not the Words

<u>I stole you</u> from your tent.

I'm not usually so impulsive, but your eyes—one hazel and one green—were so beautiful I couldn't help myself. You never actually saw me, not then. Not while you zipped your tent shut or while you lay down on the top of your sleeping bag because that night was humid. Not until my hands were in yours, my body against your body, pulling you outside with strength I only have in those moments. Strength for taking humans. I am otherwise made of slim bones, pale white skin, and red fur. A fox who is sometimes a girl.

You weren't like any other human I had taken before.

You didn't speak with your mouth; instead you used your hands. Your family, who seemed to have coerced you into their camping trip high up in the White Mountains, didn't sign with you. But I knew of your hand language because of the way you used it with your friends in video chats on your phone when you were able to find a signal. You used every muscle in your face to add layer upon layer of inflection to the movements of your hands. The conversations kept cutting out, so you sometimes punched the side of a tree in frustration. I apologized for you, but I didn't have to—even the trees understood: blood relatives surrounded you, but you were alone.

We steal people like you.

Humans who don't just feel alone but are isolated. In a group of people, you go unseen like a fae creature, like a spirit. It's easier this way. Not only because your friends and family don't notice your absence at first. You're our kindred and you don't even know it. You ache for the magic only we can give you. The songs of trees and rivers. The lives of animals up close, sometimes right against your skin. Stars reflected in pools like so many shiny fish. A sky filled with bats and the unnoticed wings of the fae, blending in with the background, as we always do.

I stole you because I fell in love with your eyes and the voice you kept in your hands like the glow of a firefly. Words I could understand better than spoken English. Not words— meanings. The way your dark hair always got in your face. The way you moved through the trees without caring what you were stepping on or how loud your steps were. I wore my fox skin during the day and I watched you, listening to the snapping of the branches under your feet as you walked away from your campsite and back, away and back. I felt the tension between you and your kin like a tightrope you walked with your arms out like wings. I don't know how you crossed that line, back and forth, so fluidly, without stumbling. I wasn't sure I could have done it, not like you.

I had to wait until nightfall before I could take you without anyone else seeing. Lucky for me, your tent faced the dark grove of hemlocks, away from the campfire and the circle of voices who didn't seem to care that you couldn't hear. I shifted under the hemlocks: my red fur became a long mane of tangled russet, my small breasts stayed hard against my skin, my nipples perked up from the chill in the late summer air, my human ears pointed up ever so slightly. The only part of me that stayed exactly the same was the amber in my eyes that matched the color of my fur and hair.

I knew my own beauty. I couldn't take humans so easily if I didn't have it.

You didn't hear me unzip the opening in your tent, nor did you hear me slip inside and take you in my arms. Once we touched, I knew it would be easy. Your skin sang against my skin as if it finally found something it had been looking for desperately.

It's not always that simple, the stealing of humans.

Sometimes they fight the connection. They reach for their gadgets: the material possessions their inner psyche understands it is losing. Instead of reaching for their lives themselves, they covet the things inside them. It becomes hard for them but effortless for me. I don't care about how pretty they are then—their souls are full of greed and plastic. It's not an asset to our realm. It's nothing that would make a good fae. Those are the humans that I take and I find a way of dissolving them. Of turning them into so many grains of sand at the bottom of a pond. Or I let them stay human. I let them go back to those objects they worship, the clothes they drape over themselves like capes, the phones they clutch in their small hands, the paint they smear on their faces. Humans like that—they think they're witches, but they're slaves.

Other times there are people like you: the human I stole from a tent in northern New Hampshire on the eve of the August full moon. You were perfect.

As soon as I released your body by the shore of the pond in the moonlight, you pulled off your clothes and dove into the shining waters. You thought I was a girl.

"Who are you?" you signed.

I understood you, but I couldn't sign back. I could only mime things that made you laugh at me, or stare in wonder at my eerie accurateness, or nod with comprehension of the meaning behind the words. You understood me, too. I loved you more for that.

We spent the night dipping in and out of the gray waters, walking the Moon's path along the shore of the pond, watching the deep green pine trees sweeping themselves back and forth over the stars. I spoke with you of fae things I had never told a human before, all with my hands making shapes, my face learning to move in the subtlest ways. Your hands were on fire with language and stories, telling me of school and home, your friends, your parents, your dog. I loved that your dog was closer to you than your family— that he was your family. But then he was gone, and you would always be broken inside. I heard things from your hands that made my fae heart ache and my skin yearn to shift back into the fox skin—into the mind that wouldn't quake at such emotions, the mind that would sort them out and follow the scent of the nearest food, slinking through the trees like a red shadow.

Your life made me cry. You kissed me.

For the first time in my life, I wasn't prepared. I couldn't do it. I couldn't make you like me. I loved you for who you were already. A human.

But a fox girl and a human?

It would never work.

I could have kept you, but I didn't. I put you back with a quiver in your heart and a dream in your head of a naked girl in a pond. The next day you and your family packed up and left.

I always wonder if I chose wisely. If sending you back to your world was the best possible thing for both of us. I wonder, but I don't let it change me. I remain a fox by sunlight and a girl by moonlight. A wanderer. And now—a lover of signed languages. Taken: hundreds of humans. Loved: almost half of them. Deeply loved: five.

Sometimes I wonder what that means about humans. Sometimes I wonder what that means about me. It's the meaning that's important, not the words used to describe it.

We've got to let the things we love go. I at least know that.

But every eve of the August full moon, I return to that pond and I wait for you.

Nang Tani

<u>I stole you</u> from the temple.

A crescent moon hung low in the sky. The monks laid out little candles all along their walkways so that visitors to the temple would not trip and fall in the dark. You walked by the golden Buddhas in your best clothes before kneeling at the back and praying with your head down low. You stood and walked slowly down the meditation path behind the temple, past the small man-made pond, past the white stupa, past the homes of the monks, until you reached my tree.

I am Nang Tani and my home is this wild banana tree you came to see. I've lived here for so long, I don't remember if I've ever had another life, but sometimes I wish I did. Sometimes I wish to be human like you and be able to go to the markets and buy fresh fruit or go to the city and take a bus somewhere.

When you reached my tree, I stepped out from the wide green leaves in my green top and skirt wrapped around my green-tinted skin. I had a red flower in my long hair. I watched you light incense as an offering to me at the base of my tree. You tied a beautiful orange silk ribbon around my tree to add to the yellow and pink ribbons I already had. I felt gratitude for those things.

You were not someone I wanted to harm.

As you stepped back from my trunk and turn to leave, I became desperate. *Couldn't you stay a little longer? Couldn't you sit down and be with me for just a while?*

I moved in front of you to stop you from leaving, but you didn't see me.

You walked through me like a ghost.

I floated back to my tree, wrapped my arms around it, and sobbed. For days, I felt lost to the world. I couldn't connect with anyone else who came to see me. People came and left so quickly. My life was an empty stretch of space between one visitor and another. A gap of time where I sat and watched the sky change from day to night to day, watched the monks attend to the gardens between my tree and their temple, watched the birds land on the white stupa and fly off again.

How I wished I could be a bird instead of a tree spirit.

Or a human. I especially wanted to be able to dance on a stage with makeup on my face and beautiful, shiny costumes adorning my body. I wanted to dance and make everyone smile.

I wanted to be free.

But people came and went as predictably as the days and nights.

❧

Weeks passed, and finally, you returned on the night of a half moon.

I hadn't singled you out for anything particular. There was nothing unusual or remarkable about your dark eyes and hair, your small frame and the simple clothing you chose to cover it. In a crowd of local people from the villages around my tree, you wouldn't have stood out at all. You'd blend in with everyone.

The reason I felt kindred to you was because you had an invisible disability. I didn't know it myself until you had come to see me a few times. A monk came up behind you once while you were walking on the path and he startled you. Another person tried to speak to you and it was clear that you didn't hear or understand their words.

When I saw that, I wondered if you felt as alone as I did with my tree. I wondered if there was a way for both of us to be together.

Every time you came to me, I stepped out from my tree. I approached you, but you looked straight through me. You didn't see anything besides my tree with the silk ribbons tied around its trunk.

I was frantic. I don't remember ever crying so much in my entire existence. Discovering you, desiring you, made me lonelier. It didn't make sense to me.

One night the moon was so full it shone like a white sun in the dark sky. The stars faded around it. Even the candles around the temple, usually bright and fiery, seemed muted in the wake of such a moon. It gave me hope.

You approached my tree once again with an offering of incense and a small handful of sweets. This time when I stepped in front of you, your eyes widened and you stepped back. You made a sign with your hands again and again.

You were signing my name. *You saw me! You knew me!*

I was overjoyed, but when I went to embrace you, you fell backwards to the ground.

I stopped. I wasn't sure how to sign, so I tried to gesture that I only wished you well, I only wished to sit with you. I sat down between you and my tree and I waited.

Your ragged breath slowed down. You sat cross-legged and stared at me. I couldn't read your face.

I waited once again, wishing for some kind of friendship or something between us. I only wanted to connect with someone, you see. But soon you stood up and bowed low to me before turning to go.

I couldn't let you leave me again. I couldn't bear the light of that full moon illuminating my solitude. I didn't choose my life. I was not like the monks of the temple. I couldn't stay with my tree forever if *this* was what forever meant.

I grabbed you from behind. I wanted to be kind. I only wanted to hug you.

But you fought against me, your arms flayed around, and I heard the sound of you trying to scream but it was as if your scream was caught inside your throat and you didn't know how to release it properly. I took your face in my hands and pressed my lips against yours.

I kissed you sweetly, but you didn't stop struggling.

I had to hold you tighter and tighter.

The loving embrace I had in my mind dissolved as quickly as your body weakened. I knew I might be hurting you. I knew I was clutching for something that wasn't mine, something you didn't want to give me, and to be honest, I hated myself for it. I hated that I needed you so badly I squeezed the life out of you.

I didn't realized I had killed you until you went slack in my arms, your head fell back, and your eyes stared blankly at the moon behind my shoulder.

A sob caught in my throat like your screams. I felt such a deep sorrow that I couldn't even cry anymore. I sank to my knees and held you while the moon crossed the sky and set behind the palm trees on the other side of the temple.

I lay beside you in the dark until another trapped spirit appeared out of the woods.

She was the floating head of a woman with her organs dangling down from her neck in a thick wet tangle. Her name was Krasue and I knew she was hungry from the way she sniffed at your body even though you were not bleeding. She usually followed the scent of blood and killed chickens or wild wounded animals. But maybe she didn't find enough of them to eat that night.

I usually felt bad for her. She was one of the spirits I used to remind myself that my fate was not *that bad*. At least I was not a severed head with my organs hanging down from my neck. I also floated and I couldn't walk, but *at least* I still had feet. I resembled a human girl.

She looked at me with an air of challenge. She knew I wasn't a killer like her, but because of that, she also knew you were more rightly hers than mine.

I wanted to fight for you. I did.

But I was tired and my loneliness rose up around me like a cage.

I slipped back to the arms of my tree as I heard her ripping your flesh and slurping up your blood. I closed my eyes and held my face against the leaves.

When she was finished, she sighed with pleasure and floated away.

I drifted out from my tree as the sun rose.

I collected your bones and bloodstained clothes.

Behind my tree in the brush, I built a small altar for you.

I lit incense beside it and gave you half of my sweets.

The Vampire from Vondelpark

<u>I stole you</u> from the fountain in Rembrandt Square.

You were smoking a joint like you always did there. Your slim fingers pressed it against your thin lips for a moment, and held it down by your leg, indiscreet the way most people smoke joints in this city. It's legal but not everyone approves. It's easier to avoid trouble by doing it inconspicuously in a park or standing by a canal. Not many people do it right in Rembrandt Square here in Amsterdam, but the tourists are so busy taking photos of the statues that most people don't notice what others are smoking along the stone benches in the square, or by the fountain shaped like a giant tan and brown rock. It wasn't breathtaking like other fountains I have seen—but that's what made it an easier place for me to live and watch people.

I watched you from inside the water, invisible to everyone who wasn't looking for something more than the plain looking rock, a place to toss a Euro for luck, a place to sit and listen to the soothing sound of flowing water. I waited a long time until there was hardly anyone around you. The only people in Rembrandt Square was a group of smiling Japanese tourists standing in front of the statues with their cameras on selfie sticks.

I reached up through the spread of water over stone and pulled you down under the soft flow of my liquid world.

Once I have a human being like you in my hands, I can make your body do anything. I myself don't fully understand it. It's like, once I touch you, my energy covets the energy controlling your body and then I have that control over you. Even your bones. I can stretch you, break your bones into pieces or turn them to jelly—to something flexible so that you can slide down the pipes with me to where they spill out into the canal.

Then I hold you against the stones and feed.

No one sees this happen. I'm alone down here beneath the fountain. Alone in the pipes. Like you, like any human creature, I must eat to survive. And I didn't get to choose the things that sustain me.

You taste like cinnamon, cloves, and weed. It's the weed I crave now. Lately everyone I've stolen from the fountain has had a joint in their hands. I'm selective like that. You just taste better. I look for other things, too. A look in your eyes. A hunger. The way your eyes shift. Guilty. Humans always have guilt in their eyes when they've done something cruel. Maybe you stole something. Maybe you hit someone. Maybe you just broke someone's heart. Whatever it was—I look for that in a person's eyes. It's the only way to be fair.

Some of my kind steal children, but I'd never do that. I'd never feed off innocence. I was innocent once.

Long ago I was born in sunlight.

I ran through Vondelpark like the wind ruffling the

leaves on the arching branches of the willow trees. I ran on legs, not the long muscular body of an eel. Not like the way I am now. I still have my old face, my beauty, but long ago when I was young, I smiled. I dreamed.

All I have is nightmares and my hair has completely fallen out. I'm bald, but I still have my round lips, my kind eyes, my small nose, my neck, my breasts. Long ago I covered the body that is now naked and I played. I ran through trails in the park, down the wide streets of the city, across the canal bridges. I ran with a skip in my step. I didn't know of the things in the sewers.

Yet, just like that, I was sucked into the water by something else. A fae or demon. Something with a very long tail. I never saw their face—only teeth. White, blood-stained teeth. And I became something else: a mutable, snake-like body. A girl with the tail of an ugly brown eel. A creature that moves through the canals and the pipes under the city. Alone.

I almost died before I discovered that I could feed.

I could dig my own teeth into you and feel healthy again. I could stop the hunger ever so briefly with the taste of you. Its memory, the memory of the taste of you, can sustain me for a while. I feed and live—watching the sunset over the curved pathways of water lined with bicycle wheels in this fabulous city. This place of art and love and drugs it both does and doesn't want to be known for. Amsterdam is more than any one characteristic. Its old arms spread wide along the sea, embracing it with stones and boats.

I love my city almost as much as I love the people who are drawn to it, people from all over the world. They're unusual. They're rebels. They're hopeful. They're athletic.

They're dreamers.

I feed on so many, I usually don't take notice of one more than another. I'm too busy trying to forget what I am. I barely stay in my body when I feed. I can't bear it. I hate to steal things.

But you—there's something in the way you move, how small and thin you are, yet your confidence is as strong as an old oak. Like how little dogs always act as if they're ten times larger. You puffed up your chest, even in the pipes. You challenged me. You fought in a way most humans don't bother to fight. You'd never be okay again. I had already stretched you and fit you down in the pipes—you couldn't have survived much longer than I would have let you anyhow. Humans can be stretched, but there's no way to shrink them back. Most of them die of shock long before my teeth find them.

So I've got to finish them off.

I've got to kill you whether I admire you or not.

But what if I did that and then fed you? Would you be able to stay with me? Feed with me? Live with me? I would not be alone anymore. I would have a friend. A companion. Someone to love. A reason to wake up in the morning besides myself. A reason to stop hating my body, hating this thing I've become.

I don't have a lot of time.

The sunset is long gone. I have you in my arms in the darkness against the side of this canal. I hear people wandering past us and the boats creaking on their dock lines. Your breath has been faltering since the fountain, but now it stops. Every other sound seems to stop with it.

Waiting for my decision. Waiting for me to choose.

I could drink and release you. That would be the way I've always done it. That would be easy. I touch the pale skin of your shoulders, your bleeding neck. The blood has caked already. I wash it off with the canal water, floating while holding your body, because I can't drown. I've got no legs anymore, I must crawl on my hands and tail or swim, but hey, I can't drown.

I open your mouth. I bite my wrist and offer it up to your lips.

After a moment, you drink.

A Real Dog

<u>I stole you</u> with a look of sweet desperation in my deep brown eyes.

My soft ears lifted ever so slightly above the top of my head. My head tilted to the side. My tiny paw pressed against the cage. I wanted to be free and *there you were!* Crouched in front of me, a baby yourself—a child staring into my eyes, maybe seeing the real me behind them, maybe not. But you were mine from that moment. All mine.

Your mother said no. Then she said yes. Your father said no. Then he said yes. You were like me in that way. You could make your parents do anything with a certain look in your eyes, your hands clasped together, your feet jumping up and down on the ground. You could do that with your parents.

I can do that with every human being I meet, especially children.

You were special, though. I could tell. I looked into your brown eyes and I saw inside them something inhuman, something fae. I had so little time left. I wanted to spend it with someone like you.

Humans don't know this, but some of them have a tiny bit of fae blood inside them. It can't be helped really. Sometimes people have sex with fairies and they can't get pregnant just from that, but when they do have a child later on, there's a little bit of fae inside the child. It gets passed down to another child. It's not enough for any of them to shapeshift or become a fairy completely, but it's enough for one of us to notice it inside one of them. It's enough for them to see things in the woods they might not otherwise see.

I wasn't supposed to be in that shelter on the day you walked in with your mother and father. I was trapped. Stuck in the body of a dog. Not just a dog—a mixed breed, a mutt the shelter personnel labeled "lab mix." I had been too wild, I killed the wrong people, and so I was cursed to live out the rest of my life as a dog as punishment. They left me in a kill shelter, fully aware that if no one adopted me, I would die.

I rode home in the back of your parents's blue station wagon. I leaned my head over the back seat so I could poke my nose out your window. The air smelled of spring flowers, grass, other dogs, and the sweat of humans running, walking, and riding bicycles. Every scent told me a story I could read at lightning speed. One after another. I couldn't believe it! Dogs get all this from sticking their head out of a car? What happened when they went into the woods? Why didn't their heads explode from all this information?

I wasn't the kind of fae who shifted and could smell things like that. I was an Irish fairy, a stealer of children. But even in the fae world, there's order. It's not just all chaos and parties with stolen children. There are always people you can't ever touch and I was stupid. A silly young fairy who took a pair of children who were so untouchable, they were practically made of gold. And my family, all the fairies I had known for ages, turned on me. They banished me across the sea to America of all places—to a kill shelter in Rhode Island.

You brought me home to a wide-open backyard with a hill and a few tall trees beyond. "That's Eliza, the season tree," you whispered into my ear and pointed at a tall oak just beyond the back corner of your brown wooden fence, "I call her that because she always tells me what season it is."

I couldn't say anything in response, so I licked your hand. You did seem to have some fae in you, though upon observing both your parents, I couldn't figure out which one gave it to you. Both of them seemed to love animals and nature but they didn't give off any sort of fae energy.

I let the mystery of it go to practice running across the expanse of your yard from end to end. I tripped and fell over on my face, getting dirt up my nose with another thousand stories of skunks and foxes and rabbits crossing that dirt over time, that exact place between one patch of grass and another, and a part of me wanted to stay there for hours just sniffing the ground but I heard you calling so I kept running.

You liked to chase me.

Already, we could run round and round together and fall down in a pile. You stuck your tongue out like mine while taking deep breaths, totally unaware that I was actually sucking up more stories about the animals of your neighborhood. Things you could never read with your tongue. There was a wild cat that I wanted to chase so badly, but she hadn't been around in a long time and would now smell my scent in the yard. Maybe she would never come back. A fox was nearby, too, but he rarely entered that square of open space your father built his wooden fence around. I wanted to share these things with you because you loved all animals, not just me, but the only sounds I could manage were barks and whines.

Days turned into years.

I watched you grow tall. I watched you play in the yard with your friends. You dressed me up for Halloween every year and placed a party hat on my head for New Year's Eve when all of your cousins came over and your grandmother watched you while your parents went out to parties. I never realized that a dog's life could be fun.

As time passed, I began to forget about Ireland. I stopped dreaming about the rolling green hills, the sheep, the crashing waves on gray rocks, the children I stole. The glittering beauty of a grove of oak trees with their branches laced together, where we used to leap and whirl, where we sang songs and ate wild berries long into the nights.

I lost my last memories while you were still young—about eight or nine, I suppose.

They held the faces of those two children. Royalty. They had blue eyes, freckles across their cheeks, and red hair down to their waists. Twins. I was so happy to steal twins. I held their tiny hands in mine. I brought them over to the place of streams and mist, woods as old as time itself, the grove where we danced. As soon as a human child sets their feet down in that place, they can never go home. They're gone from the human world forever.

My last memory of those twins was their wide eyes once they knew what it meant to follow a fairy into the woods. To cross a barrier that couldn't be crossed again.

They weren't afraid like other children. They didn't cry out or try to run. They just gave each other a secret smile and began to dance like us. They spun round and round until the other fairies came and saw who they were and saw me dancing alongside them.

Then everything went black.

I woke up in a cage, feeling drugged and tired. I scratched behind my ears with my paws and realized I was not a fairy anymore. My beautiful form, my tattered dress of leaves, my long hair, my sparkling skin—all of it was gone.

I cried for days before you came and brought me home.

By the time you were ten, I only knew the smells of your yard, the neighborhood, the feeling of your slim arms wrapped around me, the feeling of your couch below me. It was like sleeping on a cloud! I only knew dog things and ate dog food and once caught a rabbit in the yard but when I tried to bite into it, the taste of the blood and hair and skin repulsed me. I had been trained away from my own nature by human conditioning. But through it all, I didn't mind. I was genuinely happy, even eating that crunchy dog food from a bag.

You hit me sometimes. When I couldn't do what you were trying to make me do. I didn't even mind though. I forgave you faster than you forgave yourself. You were a child and somewhere in my body, somewhere close to my dog heart, I remembered how deeply I understood children. You were impulsive. When you wanted something, there was no patience—there was only that burning desire that had to happen *in that exact moment* and not a minute later. You were so creative that if adults didn't rein you in or stop you from time to time, you might have stayed awake all night telling wild stories with your toys, or wandered off and never found your way home again, only seeking adventure after adventure.

You were convinced I was not just a dog—that I was something greater, too. I was a lover in a past life of yours. I was your brother. I was your friend from another place. I was human trapped in a dog's body. I was your soul mate.

You gave me so many love names and I claimed them all with my brown eyes locked onto your brown eyes— together. Nestled in the richness of that love story you wrote for us, I forgot that I was still going to die. Not the next year or the next, but before you were grown—I would die.

I spent your teenage years hiding behind the couch or the side of your bed because you hated your parents with such a passion that I was terrified to get between you. I never knew when you would fly off the handle at them and start screaming or throwing things. You and your mother were both deaf, but you read lips and rarely used your hands to speak. You two were chained to your voices and you never knew when you were being too loud. I don't know how your father could stand the two of you.

I didn't understand all that yelling. I heard your words,

I listened, but it seemed to me that if you all just kept your mouths shut, you'd be happy again. You could be like you were when you were six and driving home with me in that blue station wagon.

In the summer of my dying, your mind lost its sharpness.

You still hated your father for drinking, which I could never understand because in Ireland, drinking was something every man did. Every single one. Your mother nagged you so much that you ignored everything she said and drove off to spend time with your friends.

You wouldn't leave me, though.

You knew I was on my way out from the limp in my step, the fact that I couldn't race you in the yard anymore, the vomit I spilled onto the hallway carpet in small, thick piles. You were furious. You were determined to keep me alive, to keep me by your side. You brought me to concerts at a park in the city, even though all that noise and human chaos made me a little sick.

I tried to hide my weaknesses from you. I tried to lift my head and rest it on your leg and not let it be too heavy.

How strange it was—to be the stolen one.

Because in all those years when I thought that you were mine, that I stole you—maybe not your body but your heart—the truth was that *you stole me*. You took my puppy body in your arms one day and held me and you never let go. I had never known a love like that, not with other fairies, and not even with the children I stole.

I belonged to you.

I didn't want it to end.

I was trapped in a dog body, but my dog body set me

free. It made me want to live on and on as long as you lived.

It was late August when I couldn't stop gagging at night. Sometimes my little stream of yellow vomit didn't even come. Sometimes it was transparent bile that left a sour taste in my mouth. I was so hungry, but every time I ate, I threw up.

You never left my side.

I fell in and out of sleep with your human body curled beside me on the floor. You made snoring sounds. When you woke in the night, I felt your hands stroking my head, the back of my neck, down my spine, across my ribs. The pain was so strong and my body was so weak, but every touch of your hands was warm medicine.

Your parents set up the appointment with the vet.

I knew they were having me "put to sleep." I could never speak, but I always understood the words around me. You screamed at your mother. You screamed at your father. But you weren't six years old anymore. You couldn't make them do what you wanted. You were eighteen and powerless as the exact time of my death was decided.

The old blue station wagon was long gone by then. We all piled into the sporty red car your father bought a few years back. Your mother had lined the back seat with blankets. I couldn't lift my head to the window, so you lifted it for me. For the last time, you lifted me.

The air outside was warm. It was still summer, but I could smell the fall coming. I liked that one of my last smells was of the coming autumn: the leaves turning crisp, as if their insides held insuppressible fire turning them red and yellow and brown as they fell and crumpled into dust upon the Earth.

I didn't die like a real dog, you know.

In those last moments, with your hands in my fur as the vet slid the sharp point of the needle under my skin, I saw myself as who I really was—I saw my fairy body again and I saw this whole story flash before my eyes like the smells I inhaled on all of our car rides together. And it was beautiful: a dog and a child.

A fairy who stole children. Who was then stolen by a child.

I knew I'd do it all again, even though I'd have to die in a dog's body. I'd steal those twins again without a second thought—just to feel your hands in my fur, to know that, for a while, I would be yours.

Floating in the Sargassum

<u>I stole you</u> from the bow of your ship.

You went there every evening and straddled the forestay. Your companion didn't like it when you were there alone, but you did it anyway, always with a harness and halyard, so you wouldn't fall into the arms of the sea (or someone like me). It took me so long to steal you I almost gave up.

   Okay, actually no. I didn't manage to do it. Sometimes I forget that I never did steal you. But I rewrite our story every day. I tell myself I had you for one night, just one, and I gave you back. But other times I remember that the truth is: I simply wanted you like no other human I had ever seen on those long Atlantic crossings. All the other sailors were made of the same tough skin, hardened with salt and wind. You were hardened, too, but you were different.

I'd like to think it wasn't just because you were blind. But maybe that was it. Maybe that's why, when I grabbed you from your perch at the forestay, you resisted. You weren't affected by the glow of my skin, the color of my eyes, or the tangled mess of my hair. I couldn't touch you the right way. You recoiled from me and the shock of the rejection caused me to slip and tumble over the lifelines back into the sea.

You shouted for your companion and met them halfway to the cockpit, "Something grabbed me! Someone else is on the boat!"

They laughed. "That's crazy! We're in the middle of the ocean and we haven't seen another boat for hours! Unless you felt a mermaid, there's nothing else that could be here."

You turned around, studying the sea. You looked right at me. Your eyes seemed to see me—or I just wanted them to see me—and you turned again and followed your companion into the boat.

I had never been so easily pushed aside.

I asked the other sirens, though we rarely communicate, so they were of little help. None of them had ever failed to steal a human from a ship. I always felt different from them, but this time, I felt inadequate. I wasn't right in my skin anymore. I wasn't a strong siren like I thought.

For weeks, I followed your ship like a lover, watching your daily ritual of sitting at the bow right at sunset. You couldn't see it, though, could you? Were the colors passing through some dark filter behind your eyes? Were they softer then?

In the mornings, when you sat in the cockpit while your companion steered the boat, were you just feeling the warmth of each day filling up the world around you? Or was it light you were watching however you could?

I had so many questions, but sirens don't speak to humans. We only take them under the sea, kiss and hold them until they turn into fish food. It's all I knew before I saw someone like you. The life I was given.

Then you came along and made me question everything.

I've been lost since that year.

I've taken lovers, both men and women that I've pulled into the sea, allowed their bodies to merge with mine before they died, but none of them matter to me anymore. Sometimes, I just float. I let myself drift like the young turtles and sea horses in the sargassum, watching the sunlight filter through the brown clusters of seaweed, turning them gold. I saved one or two from a shark, and then I realized what I was doing. Since when do sirens save turtles?

But they were helpless, weren't they? I told myself, laughing, laughing all the while.

What the fuck was it about you that turned me into this? You wouldn't last a moment down here in the sea— not blind nor human. Why did I care?

I frequented the towns along the American shore for years. Searching for you—though I never found you. One day a sighted human was swimming and they began to falter. I couldn't tell if they were drowning or trying to drown themselves. Their efforts were so futile. Were humans really that pathetic? I didn't understand, but I couldn't stop myself from investigating and helping them ashore.

A fucking siren helped a human to the beach? The world was ending, I knew it, and I turned to duck my head down beneath the waves before anyone could catch me.

The human I saved was too fast. Suddenly, on land, he was fast. He grabbed me, and our eyes met.

"Hey, who are you?" he asked.

"Just a girl on a beach," I said with a grin.

"No—now look, I've never believed in creatures that look human but aren't human, but you—there's something weird about you. You're a mermaid! Like an actual fucking mermaid."

It was no use arguing with him, so I said, "We prefer the word 'siren.' But really, I've got to go."

"Back to drifting in the fucking water? What have you got in the water that you weren't happy with before you grabbed me?"

"Grabbed you? You mean saved you! You were going to drown!"

"I can fucking drown if I decide to drown. And if you're really a siren, doesn't that mean you're supposed to help me drown?"

"I can do whatever I want. But why were you drowning yourself?"

"I felt like my whole life was caving in and nothing mattered but everything mattered and everything I touched fell apart. I couldn't do anything right. I was depressed and I wanted it all to just fucking stop."

I never understood that the way I felt was something humans felt, too. And that boy even named it. I realized then that I was depressed, too.

The human and I spoke of this thing called "depression" until sunrise. Everything we both said made sense to each other. We decided to meet again the next day and the next. I never knew that a siren and a human could be friends.

꙳

You didn't let me take you, but sometimes when I float in the sargassum, I thank you in my mind. I thank you for not letting me steal you because it taught me how to feel longing and depression. Losing you inspired me to open myself to the things around me that I hadn't noticed before. I was able to be a friend to someone.

I realized I didn't have to be a typical siren.

I could be myself.

I could float and not drown. I could save a turtle.

I could be a friend to someone without stealing them away.

The Dream Thief

<u>I stole you</u> between your waking life and sleep.

It wasn't premeditated. I never planned for you to die. Please, if you can hear my words, if you can know my truth, maybe I'll be able to forgive myself.

This is our story:

We met during one of your dreams of lovemaking.

You had them often after surgeries on your pelvis, when the doctors told you repeatedly you couldn't have sex for weeks. It was like your body, mind, and spirit came together in a quiet, sleep-induced revolt against the recurring problems that plagued your physical body. You were so much larger than them, though. In your waking life, you were a great force of loving energy to everyone. Your blue eyes and auburn hair and slim frame embraced every person you saw, regardless of race, creed, or occupation.

You drew me to you like a moth to a flame, even though I had given up the taking of humans. I thought I was finished with humans forever.

I was an old fae, you see: a dream stealer. I lived in the dream worlds: the places on the edge of waking life, on the edges of everything. Where the air was always filled

31

with smoke, and sometimes things weren't clear until they were right in front of you. Some objects were hard like in life, but others just looked that way and when you reached out to touch them, a tree or a ball or another person, your hand would slip through them as if they were ghosts. This was—is—my world.

The orgasms you gave yourself in your dreams sent out rays of light throughout the dream world. They glittered over the nightmares other people were having—of empty rooms, raging seas, storms, and bloodshed. They provided hope and I loved to watch you in the throes of them. The ways you pleased yourself made me feel things in my spirit that had been asleep for decades. Sometimes, I imagined you were with me, that I was the reason you'd felt such ecstasy, but I never had the courage to enter your dreams or communicate with you.

For years, I protected you and never went near enough to take anything of yours. I never planned to do it. I was happy just watching your ecstasy from a few dreams away, close enough to stop any other dream thieves or succubae from harming you. Everyone wanted you, you see. You were that special.

Now here's the moment when it all changed:

I was riding a bike in a child's dream when I felt something unusual in yours. You were having sex with a beautiful woman, and quite suddenly you began having a nightmare. I felt your fear as if it was something I swallowed that closed up my throat and I couldn't breathe.

I crashed the bike and rushed to you. I had never

entered one of your dreams before. I only felt them, like stardust on the edges of my world, like an ever-present rainbow over so much dark.

When I entered your dream, it was filled with purple smoke and blood raining down. Your body was a shadow on the ground with a monster crouched on its chest. The dream thief was at least twice the size of you. It had long, crooked fangs laced with drool. Its hunchback was covered in a tangled mess of brown hair, leaves, and claws. It held you around your small waist, digging its nails into your skin while leaning over your face.

I approached too quickly.

The monster turned in surprise and slashed me across the face with its claws. (I don't have a body exactly, but in dreams, everything takes form. So when I entered your dream, a body appeared around my spirit. I don't know what I looked like exactly, but in your dream I could be harmed as easily as you.)

Where the monster clawed my face, blood ran down. Through the flowing blood, my eyes met yours. I knew your eyes were blue, but in that moment, I saw every shade of every color there. I saw the promise of a thousand loving embraces from you. The real kind, the kind of love people rarely give because it scares them even more than the monster sitting on your chest, crushing the life out of you.

I leaped onto his back. I wasn't a strong fae like him. I don't know to this day how I did it, but I have to believe that I got most of my strength from you, from the look in your eyes.

He threw me off but like I said, in the dream world, the edges aren't solid. Nothing is *really* solid. Objects that feel solid at first can crumble in your hands at any time like grains of sand. Our dream bodies can crumble, too.

He slipped. He fell through the ground, taking his purple smoke and blood with him.

The following night I couldn't stay away. I found you in a grove of autumn beech trees shining like muted gold. You were naked except for a green sweater.

"Was it you last night?" you signed without opening your mouth or using your voice.

I wasn't sure if you were deaf in life or if you learned sign language from a deaf friend. It didn't matter, though. In dreams, everything is fluid, and everything speaks the same language depending on the dream. Deaf people can speak and hear in languages they've never even seen in their waking lives. Hearing people, too. Sometimes people don't use vocal or hand language; sometimes they use their bodies like animals or read the minds of beings they encounter. I don't fully understand where the dream world and the waking world meet or how or where the dream world even exists. I just move inside it, from one dream to another, one being to another.

"Yes," I answered in your hand language.

"Thank you. I think you saved me," you signed and embraced me before I could move my hands or keep my distance.

I had never made friends in dreams. I took things from people. Things like bikes or balls, and I used these small tokens as my sustenance. As a way to steal tiny pieces of dreams without hurting the person. Sometimes I made children cry, but it was nothing like that monster who almost killed you or vomited so much fear into your mind that you lost your grasp on reality and would never again function in your waking life. You—might never have smiled again. The human who brought so much joy to everyone you met.

I held back as you wrapped your arms around me, but your body was so warm, your love so deep, even for me, even for a lowly dream thief like me. I had to taste you. Just a little. I moved against you slowly at first and then faster. Your green sweater dissolved into sparkling dust, like the dust of fairies, and we were covered in it. I lay you in a bed of the softest moss and began kissing you from your neck down to your toes. I closed myself up, the power I have to steal, and sealed it away.

At first my plan worked. I was able to give you orgasm after orgasm in that beech grove, surrounded in gold and green and the pink of your blushing skin, your parted lips I bit with my teeth ever so gently. I loved you better than any human could love you, this I know. This consoles me.

We met for years, though eventually, I lost track of my time with you. I was hundreds of years old. Our time together was so brief but it was rich like Indian silk. I suppose all beings need repose. A time of rest and only love. We gave that to each other.

Things changed when your waking life partner died.

Your light grew dim despite how much I tried to nurture it, to keep you happy at least in dreams. I couldn't enter your waking life. I couldn't see how each day exhausted you. It enraged me. The powerlessness of my situation. So I began to leave you sooner and sooner each night. I moved a few dreams away and stole things people held close to their hearts. I made more children cry than I ever have, though I never killed them. I just stole things. I got stronger while watching the dim green of your light fade through the smoke.

One night I left after only a few moments. You were sad, but you didn't ask me to stay. You didn't care what happened in your dreams then. You just drifted through them like a speck of fairy dust that used to be a fae being itself. You didn't even use dreaming for respite anymore.

My chest tightened.

I was so many dreams away from you—so far—when I heard you scream, that I kept falling through the smoke. I kept slipping through the ground.

Every dream I tried to cross to reach you was a valley of quicksand. Thick mud covered me in brown. I couldn't move fast. I could barely take one step and then another.

Finally, I reached that grove of beech trees and the leaves were gone. The trees were gray skeletons twisted in mourning. Your ravaged body lay on the dead moss, as brown as the fallen leaves, crystallized over in frost. Your mind had been shattered. I knew it without even touching you.

When I did lay my hands on you, I felt you in between the dream and your waking life. Your body was softer, fading away. I couldn't let you leave like that. I couldn't let you wake up into a life of madness.

I took you in my arms before you melted away. I brought my lips down against yours and stole the rest of you. I took your mad energy into my body and you disappeared. So quickly, you were gone from the world of dreams and life. A rainbow fading to black. I was left in the grove of beech trees crumbling brown leaves into dust around me, waiting for winter.

A Murder of Two

<u>I stole you</u> in the pouring rain.

The air was cool but not cold. The leaves had lost their fire and were falling from the trees in swirls of brown stars. Your hair was red, a dusky deep shade close to that of human blood when it reaches the air. You were running down the empty black street lined with elms, birches, and maples; old, twisted trees with cracked bark covered in pale green lichen and moss.

For a minute, I thought you were someone else. A human I stole many years ago, in a time when this place was torn from civil war. When bodies lined the dirt roads, their blood caked to their faces and arms. Sad lines of buttons shining in the sunlight on their chests that will never rise again. The costs of disagreement, of thinking differently, of politics. It matters little that I kill some of you.

It matters little because you kill yourselves so much better.

War is starting again.

None of you know it, of course. You silly humans, running down your dark streets toward a deeper darkness than you've ever seen. I save each human I take, because I stop you from seeing that—I stop war for you and leave you with kinder memories of your brief lives.

My body is covered in black feathers. It's a body like yours, but I can shift into a much smaller form and fly off across the fields of corn with the crows. They don't always notice how different I am until I shift and enlarge, and immediately upon seeing my human-like form covered with feathers and my giant beak, they fly off. A murder of crows, sometimes over a hundred of them. I like to watch them fly in such large numbers. They fill up the sky.

So many of you people would like to have wings. You've told me as you were dying, and sometimes I've carried you in my arms and tried to fly in my large form. I failed every time. But I occasionally jumped so high, you felt as if you were flying for a moment. That made me very happy.

My victim from long ago—the one with the red hair the exact shade of yours, the tall, thick body—was a challenge because I am tall, too, but I am not strong. I don't use force to suppress my victims. I use my face, my feathers against their skin, my feathers all around them. Confusing is the best way to dismantle a human. I steal your ability to think logical thoughts. I steal your ability to escape.

The other human was my first.

I was a young crow fae then. A weightless bird with her head in the clouds. I thought it would be romantic, but really, I just pecked out his eyes. They tasted sweet and warm, and the man's screams didn't bring anyone rushing to check on him because it was a time of war, because there was already a background of screams and gunshots and rain. I love to kill in the rain. The water washes the blood away. It washes my own body afterwards, like a cleansing. I feel clean again and ready to fly for a long time before my next kill.

My first human's energy lasted me for fifty years. I flew all over the world without stopping. I flew round and round. I like to think that I've seen everywhere there is to see. Every one of your countries with their vastly different cultures, their cruelty, their inability to live harmoniously with other groups of themselves nor with animals. Your passions, your mind-less egos. You're like birds with your chests puffed out. You're as weak and fragile as me, but you think you're not. That's your downfall.

My first human thought he could cross a field of men shooting at each other. He was strong and fast, but it wasn't enough. Gunfire continued long after he fell to the ground riddled with holes. I flew to him and dragged him away from the field so that I could feed under cover of the trees.

Like I said, I first pecked out his eyes. Two jewel candies slid down my throat. Then the bullets. One by one, I gathered them up in my beak and spit them out into the dirt. I licked his skin. I licked all the blood mixed with rain until he stopped bleeding, until the rain stopped, too. I pecked one hole after another into his soft flesh. I gulped each piece of his skin down. With my beak, I absolved him of more judgments. No more struggles. That human was finally free when he was turned into bones scattered over moss.

The woods around us are quiet except for the sound of the drops falling down, pooling in small rivers alongside the empty street. You're running and your face disarms me because it seems to be the same face as my first human from years ago. I don't understand it. I don't believe you can come back in another body. Not at all. But maybe—maybe you have ...

I rush into you, a swarm of giant feathers tickling you until you breathe them in and they suffocate you. I drag you into the trees.

Once again the trees act as a refuge for me, a safe place to do as I please out of sight. When I kill you from the holes I make in your skin, you even taste like my first. The same sweetness is in your blood, too. I lick until I have eaten all of your flesh. I leave your bones lying clean and washed upon the fragments of your clothes.

I peck your skull fondly, because of how wonderful you tasted for the sweat that made you taste saltier yet richer at the same time, and for the blue of your eyes, allowing me to imagine I was eating the sky itself, even though the sky above us was gray. I imagined the blue, clear sky inside your eyes and I ate it in two gulps. I was connected to everything the sky touched. Everything on Earth.

It was only for a moment, but the moment lasted and lasted in my head. I played it over and over while I flew across the Atlantic Ocean, south over Africa, and east over Asia and across the Pacific, and over the Panama Canal and the islands beyond. I flew while your energy, the memory of your killing, sustained me for another fifty years.

Don't ask me where humans went after your death or where they ended up.

I refuse to tell you the end.

You'll never know it, but your children might and their

children most certainly will know. Your end isn't pretty like the way that I ate you: bent down low, my wings sticking out behind me causing me to appear like a harmless duck leaning over you and pecking. Endlessly pecking chunk after chunk, licking the dripping red in between, licking the sweat from your skin. I ate until I couldn't eat anymore. I cleaned and laid out your bones like a fortune teller divining the future of your kind.

I was wrong. Ever so wrong.

Humans, you've surprised me.

You've burned weakly and irritably in the dark until the Moon rose in the sky, and you turned the moonlight into gold for a while.

But nothing gold can stay, can it? You were rigged from the start. You lived and you died. Young. Wild. Selfish.

The Art Lover

<u>I stole you</u> from the café.

It took years. I first noticed you in the fall. You wore Doc Marten shoes and stripes on your clothes, usually black and white or black and red. Your hair color changed from week to week. I liked your style. You didn't follow any trends; you started them, though you never noticed it. You never saw your surroundings in that way. You saw beyond the patterns of current cultural fashions or panaches. You were an artist. A painter. And within weeks of meeting you, I couldn't stop going back: to the café, to the table where you sat.

"Hi, how are you?" I said because that was how people spoke to each other, quickly, as if they didn't really want to hear a response or even greet each other in the first place.

"Hi," you mumbled and buried your face in your work.

It was a sketch of the barista. Then a pastel drawing of the small circular table in the window with two women leaning close together over it, their faces almost touching, their hands entwined. One was black and the other was Asian. You watched them kiss and smiled a secret sort of smile, as if you were gay, too, or wanted to be, or maybe you just thought their gestures were beautiful on their own.

I liked your lack of judgment. I liked your shyness. I liked the way you held your pencil and the pastels. You lifted each instrument up to your mouth in between strokes as if you were deep in thought, never just drawing something blindly.

"I love your work," I said.

You didn't respond.

"Your pictures are awesome," I said, slightly louder and more in line with young people's way of thinking.

I look about sixteen. I usually can convince people I am twenty-one when I have to, so I have the freedom to shift between age groups, between teens and adults, and play with everyone. I love to tease people into revealing their worst fears and then if I like them, I only give them the easiest ways to die, but if I hate them I wait until I can orchestrate the most terrifying way to die for a specific person and that's how I steal them. That's how they die, exactly like their worst fears.

I liked you from the start, but I was hungry. I never balked at the thought of taking you, even though I liked you and I felt like I could watch you draw for years. You were showing me a window to another way to see reality, and one rarely gets that now—with anyone, in any animal group. You can never really get close enough to another creature, not all the way into their minds. Except through creatures who are able to produce art. Those kinds, humans and whales, for example, can show you the most beautiful and the most ugly things. Things you'd never imagine on your own and couldn't render yourself.

I once followed a blue whale for centuries, just listening to his song. It broke my heart.

I liked you, but the closer I got, the less I wanted you to die, which was frustrating because I was hungry. But I tried. I tried to stop eating for you—to spend time with you.

"Hey!" I finally said and waved in your face.

You looked up surprised, and that's when I realized—you hadn't heard me. You were deaf.

"Oh," I signed, "I didn't know you were deaf," in American Sign Language, because I learn every new language humans create as it happens.

In my most natural form, I am formless. I am air. But I can shift into anything alive.

I spent over a hundred years as a banyan tree in order to learn about connecting branches back down with roots, about how the end can come back and meet the beginning.

I spent nearly a century as an elephant, to learn about loyalty, love, and strength of spirit. Did you know that elephants love the deepest out of all the animals?

I spent two hundred years as a dolphin to learn about joy. Not the kind humans show, which is learned from their elders and confines within their social behavioral norms, but the joy of a heart free of everything, so at one with their body that they can move it masterfully, soaring through the sea in a way closer to birds than sea mammals. Dolphins know joy best of all the animals.

Did you know that you humans share so many of your emotions with animals?

But the one thing you don't share with anyone else is regret. Guilt. No other creatures, fae included, feel this emotion. This is your biggest weakness, yet at the same time, it has helped you produce your art so well. Your art is your greatest achievement. The beauty of your inner fantasies. The terror of your nightmares. We fae only make your dreams and nightmares come true because you've already created these things in your minds. Isn't that brilliant of you? How you've contained yourselves by your stories. How you live them out again and again, always in some small way due to regret.

"How do you know sign?" you asked in an ASL that followed more closely with the English language, so I knew you had surrounded yourself with mostly hearing people and that you used English more than ASL, though you needed the signing to help you understand what people said.

You also felt regret.

From the way you moved your hands, I read that you regretted not being able to sign better and not having fluent signers around you. You lived between hearing and deaf cultures, and I think that was why your art was different. It said things other pieces of art didn't say because you were more familiar with these cracks in the world, the spaces between things—not just hearing and deaf cultures, but that familiarity gave you a deeper understanding of how it is for all things in between.

Your art spoke to me because I am also in between. I shift between forms all the time. I've only been human for fifteen thousand years now, and sometimes, for a week or two, I shift into other animals like a fox or a dog. I sneak through the woods, smelling the richness of dirt, the remains of deer or field mice, learning their stories, keeping track of what's going on with other creatures beyond humans.

I keep shifting back to this form: a girl of sixteen who can fake twenty-one, a girl with long blond hair I like to keep tied back to make me look more subdued, a girl with a short, unthreatening frame to make me look weak, a girl with brown eyes to make me look kind. I've worn all kinds of clothes, but right now, I like to wear flowered short dresses, thick woolen leggings, dark boots, and cardigan sweaters in soft colors like burnt orange and light blue. I am the girl you see in the café and think *what a sweet looking girl that is!* and you usually don't approach her. You usually just say hi and carry on, but you return to the café again and again, hoping to see her smile at you.

I give my smile away freely but that's all I give away.

I watch your people, and in every gesture they make, every movement of their eyes, every word they say, I don't read their minds—I read their souls. I take the ones who are closer to demon than human, because I know they bring your race down and I don't want to see your end. I want you to go on forever, just so I can collect your art and live off of that nectar. It makes me less lonely.

I only eat artists. Writers, too. It gives me more sustenance than the consumption of other animals because of the beauty and color of their brains. You must understand this—if you eat what you love, you feel stronger and happier. I also feel less alone.

❧

"It was just something I picked up over time," I signed, not wanting to lie to you.

"Oh, you sign really well."

"Thank you. I was trying to tell you I love your work," I pointed to the sketch in your hands.

"Oh, really? I'm just getting back into it. I need so much more practice."

"You should come by my apartment sometime. I collect art and I think you might get some inspiration from the paintings I have there."

"Which artists do you have? Maybe I know them."

"Van Gogh, Frida Kahlo, Gauguin, Alice Neel, Picasso, Michelangelo …"

"What?!" You eyed my thrift-store outfit, my youth, and immediately saw the ridiculousness of my answer. "You can't possibly have originals of those artists. You must mean prints or something, right?"

"No," I knew I had to lie. "My family has collected art from the masters for generations. They're very rich. But I don't live that way now. I moved out of my parents's house a few years ago and took my favorite pieces of art. They weren't happy, but they let me do it."

"Wow, then umm, okay. Yeah. I would totally go to your apartment and check those things out. I'd love to— thank you for wanting to show me."

That was how I've gotten every artist I've ever taken.

I tried to kill Van Gogh, but he beat me to it. I was devastated. I fell in love with him. Vincent had such a troubled spirit and so much regret. I made love to him so many times I can still feel him inside me now. Anyway,

Vincent was one of my favorites. I still taste the shadow of him on my tongue. It tastes bright yellow and turquoise. Vivid orange and muted red. His colors were music for me.

Every few weeks, I lay down on my futon bed surrounded by his art and get lost in the ecstasy of the colors. I become air just so I can enter each of the paintings and feel how they were layered, how each color touched the others. In those moments, I am color. I am paint. I'm the dream of a mad artist breaking free.

I led you up the curved staircase to my fifth-floor apartment in Dover. I like to live up high where I can see as much of the town around me as possible. Whenever I can, I sit in my window each night, I watch people move between the buildings, learning so many things just from that.

You gasped when you entered my apartment, because I lived alone in a three-bedroom and every inch of every wall was covered with art. My bedroom had all my Van Goghs together, and a few of Kahlos as well. The paintings had never been recorded in history because I took them from the artists themselves, from their private collections, their studios.

"Your family was really able to collect all these?" you signed with no sign of your shock abating as you rushed through the apartment to quickly assess everything before you examined the paintings more closely one by one.

Most artists take hours before they can speak to me again from the time that they enter my apartment. All of them ask repeatedly if it is real. If what they are seeing is really what they are seeing. Your disbelief is cute. I love this part of my kills. I love it—

Yet as you made your tour, sometimes sitting down to sketch or just sitting because the talent of a particular artist had floored you, I wanted to kill you less and less.

Instead, I wanted to learn how you had come to love art. What your parents did. What you drew first when you were a child. I wanted to know the things I couldn't decipher in your gestures and eyes. The minute details I normally don't care about at all.

I did give Van Gogh, Gauguin, and Kahlo many years before I was ready to take them, because I loved them, but they had also made some of the greatest works of art before I knew them personally. You hadn't done anything yet.

After you finished examining every piece of art I owned, it was close to midnight. Neither one of us was hungry or sleepy. The art fed you as well as it fed me.

The following day I went to your apartment to see everything you had ever painted and kept. Your unmistakable talent was there, but most of the pieces were nothing special. You needed more time. But could I give that to you? Could I hold back long enough? I still wasn't sure.

"I burn some of them in the backyard," you signed with your head down, as if ashamed, "when I'm feeling like I need to just release them. Does that sound crazy?"

Compared to some of the things I saw Vincent or Frida do? No way. "Of course not," I signed. "So many artists do much crazier things."

"Oh! Like Van Gogh cutting of his ear?"

"Well—"

"What do you mean? He did do it, right?" Your blue eyes narrowed. You were testing me, but it wasn't really a test anyone could pass because no person who was alive in the world at that time knew the truth.

Except me.

"He didn't exactly do that himself. It was an accident. He was definitely crazy. But he didn't do that."

"How do you know?"

I wanted to sign, *Because I was there*, but I couldn't. So I lied, "I read in a secret letter that my family kept hidden that he and Gauguin had an awful fight and Gauguin was an expert fencer and accidentally cut off Van Gogh's ear and that ended their intense relationship. He left and Van Gogh protected his friend—or lover, according to some people—by saying he did it himself."

"No way. Wow. That's so much more interesting. Why couldn't your family share the letter with the world?"

It was so convincing. The lies I could tell with the body I chose. Everyone—male or female, rich or poor—always believes small, petite blonds. I was always trusted. "They were sworn to secrecy by Van Gogh's family. They didn't want people thinking that he was gay."

"But—do you think he was?"

Images flash through my mind: intense, beautiful ones of Van Gogh and Gauguin, of their bodies and the night sky above them. I shuddered. "Maybe," I signed.

"That would be so beautiful to me. I'm bisexual. I keep falling for anyone, it seems, but I'm just not great at keeping people around because I always put my art first."

I knew that we would be lovers. I knew I would get to see your whole body unclothed, natural. I loved that moment most. The edge of that particular precipice. Almost.

Later that night you peeled off my clothes first. I wore a simple blue hooded sweatshirt over one of my short floral pattern dresses to appear casual. I thought we might start something that night, but I didn't imagine it to be as perfect as you orchestrated it.

You put classical music on. "I was able to hear until my late teens," you explained so that I understood why you knew the best kind of music to play in the background.

We lay on your bed naked for a long time, just kissing and touching each other. When we made love, it was slow. You were taller than me and heavier. You worried about hurting me when you lay on top so we rolled back and forth. I did things that gave you orgasms that left you shaking for a long time, things I came up with only after over a thousand years of practice.

I stayed with you and woke to coffee and muffins you had picked up at the café where we met. You sketched while we ate. I knew my art and our conversations had lit a fire in you that you hadn't had in years. It was a good time to leave you to work alone for a while.

"I've got to go back home for a few days," I signed.

"Oh, where is home?"

"Minnesota," I fingerspelled. "I'll be back."

I didn't go to Minnesota, but I went to Rhode Island.

The School of Design in Providence to be exact. The artists at RISD had a lot of talent, too, and like I said, I was hungry. I couldn't take you yet. The sex had made me ravenous though.

I shifted between a deer and a fox, and ran as fast as I could across the states. I couldn't stay in human form to take a train or a bus. I would have looked crazy like my beloved Van Gogh. Eating plants and small animals in the woods sustained me a little longer.

When I reached Providence, I shifted back into my human form and entered the student studios by moonlight. A boy was painting in broad sweeping strokes with a bottle of whiskey in his hand. I could tell he was drunk by the way he was swaying on his feet.

I stepped up behind him. "That looks just like a Jackson Pollock."

He turned. I smiled at first, which made his initial surprise dissolve into a kind grin in return. "Hi," he said, "I haven't seen you here before."

"I'm a new student," I said and opened my mouth.

I opened it farther than a human mouth could go. His eyes widened as my teeth grew long and pointed, and my lips stretched out thin around jaws that became the size of my entire human face. My hands turned into claws, but he—like most of my victims—never noticed them at all.

The whiskey bottle smashed on the floor as I grabbed his upper arms with my claws and tore into his neck.

His blood tasted of paint splatters on a white canvas. Black, purple, red, and brown. I let it splatter on the floor as

I ate, knowing that by the time anyone found him, I would be a fox slinking through the woods to the north, heading back home to you.

The boy's work was a bit more abstract than I usually liked, but the size and scope of his vision filled me up. I left his bones with scattered chunks of fat and skin. The police would be shocked. Animal control would be notified and searching the city before dawn. Searching for a rabid dog perhaps. What else in Rhode Island could do such a thing?

I turned back as I slipped out the door, admiring my own art, my abstract work with only organic materials. The boy's skull peeked out at me from under tufts of his hair. I smiled as I made my way down the halls, pausing in the bathroom to wash my face and hands.

I left through the side door of the building. I ran my fingers over the red bricks as I walked down the street just far enough before shifting into a fox under a large elm tree and darting away.

When I returned to Dover, I took a long hot shower and donned another floral dress. I walked to your apartment. You were in the middle of painting something bold. I saw that my Alice Neel pieces had spoken to you. You were using photos of people, but you knew they weren't the best way to paint a particular subject. Of course, I agreed to model for you.

We made love first, so when I sat down to model, my skin was glistening with sweat. You painted that, too. You made me shine like an angel, naked with hair as yellow as a cornfield, skin blushing with pink, all the shadows and lines in deep Prussian blue.

I loved the way you saw me.

We advertised for models together, and you began doing portraits. We met in the café and I became your assistant while you set up your easel on a small table and painted friends, lovers, and families. The café offered up their walls to you, and you sold everything. That had never happened to you before. Paintings shown in restaurants hardly ever sold, but yours were so captivating that people couldn't see them more than a few times without wanting to buy one and bring it home.

Then you had a show at a gallery in Boston, like I suggested, and everything sold there, too. You were becoming a small sensation.

You excited me so much, I had to "go home to Minnesota" every week. Sometimes I left for weeks at a time so that I wasn't killing too many people in one city. I traveled to Canada, all over New York City when you were showing there, and as far as Washington, D.C. I considered turning to air and flying somewhere, but I cannot become air for very long. I need a body to stay alive.

All my life I've never known how I was born, but my first memory is air: a warm, humid breeze. Somehow I entered the largest body I've ever taken—a dinosaur with a neck so long I could eat the tops of the trees. Their leaves were so thick and juicy, but I had to eat an enormous amount just to keep my body alive and able to move across the valleys and mountains, able to strike down other dinosaurs when they attacked.

Eventually I became trees themselves and was able to rest for many years. I could live as a tree for centuries, only eating the air and absorbing nutrients from the Earth itself through my roots. I do this periodically to rest.

I wanted you to live for so much longer. You were barely in your thirties. You could have gone on to be one of the greatest artists of your generation. Do you know how many humans have that potential? More than you could ever imagine. Regret does you all in. Regret destroys you faster than a T. rex can tear through a triceratops.

I only know what I have seen, and I've seen too much. I am the oldest fae in the world.

I held you close while you sobbed. The response to your newest show, all of which was positive, had overwhelmed you. I ran my fingers along your spine. I kissed the back of your neck under your hairline.

Then I opened my mouth.

I didn't spread my lips so wide as I did for the boy at RISD. I didn't grow such long teeth. No. When I kill someone I love, I do it like a song.

I bit the back of your neck with razor sharp teeth, small ones; teeth grown to the exact length needed to create a delicate yet rushing flow of blood down your back.

"Owww," you moaned. I knew you were feeling lightheaded. The fact that you hadn't eaten all day helped. Your body was going numb and cold at the same time. You shivered against me, so I sucked harder to speed it up.

I cried, too.

Your sobs became my own and my tears mixed with

your blood, turning it pink because my tears weren't as transparent as human tears. I hardly ever cry, but when I do, I am careful not to do it in front of anyone because my tears fall like shiny white pearls, thick with memory and feeling.

When I finished, I held all the pieces of you in my arms and slept until morning, still wishing I could put you back together again.

Love within Tangled Branches

<u>I stole you</u> from the base of the old birch tree, half-lying down alongside the trail.

The moths almost didn't let me do it. They don't always agree with us. In Iceland, we're all connected—the trees, the birds, the flowers, the rivers, the stones—we communicate through touch and wind. But sometimes we don't agree. There was a flurry of wings as I reached for you. You were so enraptured with the tree that you hadn't noticed me. You didn't care that I slipped my arms around your small waist and dragged you deeper into the bushes.

When you realized that your beloved tree was no longer above you, and instead you were facing me: an elf with a face of green leaves, hair falling down in shades of white, pink, brown, and gray, you froze in shock but you didn't run.

I was a birch elf, like the one inside your tree, but my tree was hidden away farther up the mountain. I love her, but I can't stop leaving her. When I stay in my tree, I don't get the kind of attention the larger birch along the path gets and I'm jealous. I'm a small tree, so small that I can't move very far from my roots. But I can make it to the path.

I needed more sustenance. I needed you.

You didn't run when you saw what I was. You embraced me. You took my lips against your own and began to sign things to me with your hands. I didn't know how to respond, though I understood you. All elves understand humans because we read your minds while you speak or, in your case, sign. We read the vibration of your voices, the touch of your feet against the ground, the movements of your hands and arms, the tilts of your head.

I touched you with the branches in my hair, careful not to scratch you, but you pulled me in so close, some of my branches snapped against your chest and arms. You held me roughly and I knew—you were happy to be deaf. Perhaps your deafness had opened you to the trees and the wind more than other people you knew—but at the same time you weren't content in your own skin. You were as jealous of me as I was of the larger birch tree. You wanted my peeling bark, my stiff hair, my green leaf eyes.

We don't make elves from humans. That's not the way of my kind.

But you were different. *Could we do it?* I wanted to find out.

The other elves fought against us. They pulled you back down toward the open arms of the other birch.

You didn't understand. You just wanted to be one of us. A birch tree elf in Iceland. Though the time was summer and you had never seen an Icelandic winter. You didn't know about the snow and the wind. That the way my sisters and brothers were pulling you then was nothing compared to the way our winds could rip you apart in the darkness of a winter day.

❧

"Why do they pull me from you?" You asked me one day while we lay at the base of my tree with the small town and the lake spread out below us down the hill and snow-covered mountains edging the sky to the north.

"You're not supposed to be one of us."

"I should have been born a tree. I just want to stay here on this hill forever, watching this sky and this land."

"I want you to stay, too," I mimed in a mix of your sign language and my own thoughts pushed out toward you that you were starting to understand. This gave me hope. Maybe if you could learn to read my thoughts, you could become an elf like me.

Winter came and you had to get woolen clothes and a parka in order to walk up to my tree. I tried meeting you on the path, but the other elves were working with the wind so they blew me down, threatening to rip my tree out of its roots or send a tremulous crack down the center of it. They wanted to destroy the love we found within tangled branches.

One day I thought we were both going to die.

The snow was deep and cold, even for me. The wind blew so hard I had to grab hold of the branches of that first birch tree you found, the only one who gave us any sympathy, who lost you with grace and dignity. Without her, I would have surely blown down the path, down the ice river, and smashed into the road.

I saw you walking up toward me. I reached out my

hand. You reached out your hand. There was a moment when we both looked up and saw the northern lights in full glory: spread across the sky in neon greens and fuchsias. I see them every autumn, winter, and spring. Sometimes I lie against my tree, close my eyes, and feel the lights warming me despite the snow. But this time seeing those lights was different. You were so dazzled by them that I felt like I was seeing them for the first time. I remembered being so tiny, barely a sprig of a tree, and looking up at a sky on fire. You reminded me of myself, and I held onto that great lovely birth tree with new respect. I wasn't jealous of her anymore, because I had you. She had you first, but she didn't get to keep you. She wasn't right now reaching for your hand and touching your fingers. Yours were in thick mittens, but I still felt the energy of you inside them, warm and glowing like the lights above us.

And just like that, you were gone.

The other elves—or just the wind itself—blew you down the path the other way.

The birch tree, which looked like a giant waving hand, and I had a second where I could have stayed—I could have nestled myself into that hand and been made safe.

But love makes travellers and risk-takers of us all, elf and human alike. I slipped out of that great old birch tree with a warm breath of goodbye, and I let the wind take me. I followed the speck of your black hair down the hill, letting myself roll through the snow, smashing against a tree here and there. I felt my body breaking a little more with each new stretch of distance between my tree and myself. I knew I would not last long. I urged the wind to carry me faster so I could get a final glimpse of you, my love.

Everything happened so quickly that before I knew it, I was smashed against a cluster of shrubbery by the frozen lake. I looked around frantically, but I couldn't see you. I felt cold all over the bark of my skin, way down into my bones. I lay back against the rocky shore, thinking suddenly about the tree I abandoned for love. The rest of me. The roots I had dug down deep so that the wind wouldn't take me this way, the branches I had grown, stronger than they look, some of them nearly unbreakable.

I didn't know there were other things out there besides the wind and storms that could damage me. As I slipped off into nothing, I thought of your hands moving, telling me stories with their slim fingers. I wondered if you were still out there, signing with those hands, walking through the snow, alive.

Shining Orange

I stole you because you were dying so far from your family—
in the place where you spent your life on the streets saving
dogs no one else noticed.

People passed them by as if they weren't there at all. Tiny
puppies that could fit in your palms. Dogs with one leg
missing or two. Dogs covered in mange with skin full of
scales. Dogs with maggot-wound holes in their necks as
large as mangoes. Dogs that were dying faster than the
humans who also lived on those orange streets. Dogs that
lay in the dirt shining orange like the sun, waiting for no
one besides you and the handful of humans you inspired.

You didn't take assistance very well. You were stubborn.
I liked that about you. You had to be that way because the
people around you believed the dogs were not part of them.
People threw rocks. They screamed. Their cows or goats
died and always, they blamed the dogs, and eventually, they
blamed you because they saw you were with the dogs.

South India is not for the faint of heart.

I love my country. I love its colors and gods. I am
Uluka, the goddess Lakshmi's vahana, her mount. I carry
her throughout the night, though sometimes she lets me

fly on my own. I like to wander above the streets where you spent your last years riding your small moped with buckets of leftover food attached to the front. I watched you give and give to the dogs in all the villages surrounding the community built by Westerners along the Bay of Bengal.

You didn't just protect the dogs. You also protected my kind. I am an owl. Not an ordinary animal, of course, but they are still my kind. They are a part of me. The little boys of the villages often threw rocks at the smallest owls perched in the banyan trees along the roadsides at night, sometimes killing them. I've watched so many of their soft bodies fall to the dust, dying beside the dogs. Whenever you saw those boys, you screamed at them in Tamil to get away, to stop, and they laughed at you but they ran away.

I never wanted to see you die. You were no different than the dogs or the owls. You could not live beyond the limits of your body. You barely ate because you couldn't stop feeding those dogs. You barely slept and when you did, you chose the dirt floor of a storage unit or the soiled mattress of a capsule, a one-room hut elevated off the ground with a roof of palm leaves, filled with dozens of cats. You gave to every animal in need around you.

I watched you wither, worrying in a way I had never done before. Even Lakshmi didn't understand it. She let me take night after night for myself, because I couldn't stop wanting to check on you. I don't normally feel such— emotion, I suppose—for humans.

You came down with colon cancer when you were only fifty-six. You still rode everywhere on that moped with barrels of leftover food and medicine. You still gave rabies shots, cleaned out gaping maggot wounds, and applied your medicinal oils to mange-covered skin. You worked hard right up until you couldn't see straight and your friends had to drive you to the hospital for those final months.

Let me go back to the first time I saw you:

It was night and you were driving down the red roads of the universal town of Auroville with a giant barrel of extra food. Your straight brown hair was tied back away from your face. Your eyes were so blue they shone like sapphires under the occasionally working streetlights.

You felt familiar to me before I even understood that you didn't belong with other humans. You didn't look like any man or woman around you, not the Indians and not the Westerners either, who moved to that town in order to realize human unity, and part of that was perhaps because you loved the animals more. You saw their suffering. You felt it inside your own heart like a maggot wound you couldn't stop nursing.

You humans cannot choose what you love. You can only choose how you respond to it. This I have learned from so many years of watching you from the trees. Your strength of character lent more power to that wound in your heart for the animals. You had motivation like the mount of a god, like the drive I must have in order to carry Lakshmi across the sky.

Your unwavering focus piqued my curiosity. I followed you as you rode through the darkness, staying just far enough behind so that you wouldn't notice my owl body in the trees, balanced above you, my head spinning round.

From that close distance, I could feel the thoughts in your mind. *Are these dogs okay for now? Yes. On to the next.*

I'm so frustrated with my body for feeling tired right now, so I'll do one more village, one more street. There's still food left. Nothing should go to waste. I must get to the next ones. What about that dog with dysentery on the other side of town? I'll go there first thing tomorrow. Six a.m. If I get to sleep by two or three, then that should be enough time for me to rest. There is so much to do. I cannot stop now. So many things I must do tomorrow.

I was convinced you must think about yourself occasionally, but you never did. I flew on, listening to the same words in your mind pass through one after the other. Dogs. Dogs. Dogs. Cats. Dogs. You never wavered, though you sometimes thought of goats.

For over twenty years, I shadowed you relentlessly following the lists of endless tasks in your mind. Even on your birthdays, when friends urged you to take time for yourself, you responded, "Oh, not today. There's too much to be done. I'm alright."

Through your contact with the few locals who were willing to take in a puppy, you learned Tamil. "*Va, va,*" you said to the dogs, begging for them to come to your coconut shells filled with curd or raw eggs for their breakfast. "*Po, po,*" you said to the dogs who tried to steal food from other dogs. You also said "*Po*" to the human beggars, because you had one drive, like mine with Lakshmi, so there was nothing left for you to give to another creature, human or not.

You humans are not as wide as the sky or as deep as the sea. Your energies fit into cups, into glasses, and they come in all sizes but any of them can be emptied, any of them can be shattered. It only takes one wrong moment.

❧

It feels at times that I was always your shadow owl.

I was always there in the trees above your slowly moving moped, your human body that shed more and more of its weight as the years passed. That is how I learned, over the years, that I would miss too much of your life if I slept all day. I learned to sleep in the darkness above your head, in banyan trees from the hours of midnight until dawn. I learned to wake at daybreak so that I could watch you shuffle outside barely drinking water or eating some curd while feeding your cats before motoring off to the dogs.

In your final days, you finally obtained a piece of land from Auroville. It only took them over thirty years to honor your cause. It only took an American woman to fight your battles for you and fill out the forms for you to have the right to build a shelter and a hospital for your beloved dogs. And she did it not for the dogs themselves, but for you. Because she loved you, because she saw what I saw—that you were not like other humans and those dogs had no one else who would care for them so forcefully, with every ounce of sustenance you had.

By then, you were sick. You body was failing you before your dreams could ever come to fruition. If I had a feather for every time that happened in a human's life, I'd have a body the size of a million owls, a body that could cover my entire country and beyond.

The final morning you spent working in the village was full of conflict, which for you was normal. A Tamil man ran up to you as you were getting into a taxi that your friends had convinced you to take to the local hospital because you could barely stand.

He screamed, "My cow has been bitten by a dog! You must come help! It's your fault the dogs have bitten my cow!"

Your head was swimming with thoughts of how to help this man, but your body wasn't allowing you to speak. You faltered. A Tamil friend held you steady while another Tamil friend explained your situation to the man.

Their words turned to screams and you lost sense of what was being said.

In your head you thought of all the things you planned to do that day and the next. All the dogs—and now this cow—that needed your help. You grasped the door of the taxi but only to use it for standing, keeping your feet on the dirt. No part of you wanted to enter that car. Somehow, you knew that white car was the chariot of death. You felt it down in your bones, but you refused to accept it. *There's no time for me to be sick! There's no time for me to die! I've got to help the dogs!* Your thoughts raced in circles like samsara—birth, death, rebirth, birth, death, rebirth, birth, death, rebirth.

The man behind you raged, he was sweating just as much as you were, spit fell from his mouth to the orange dirt at your feet as he screamed to your back. "I will kill all the dogs in the village if you don't help me!"

Your friends, who cared more for you than the dogs, told him to go ahead and do it.

Then they pushed you inside the chariot with the brown leather back seat.

~❧~

It was the same taxicab you had taken countless times with severely injured dogs to the veterinary college in Pondicherry, where students performed surgeries and consultations for free as part of their schooling. The same cab where a dog with two broken legs tore free from his muzzle and bit you. The same cab where you were denied help from the driver or your helper, where you re-muzzled the dog that was blind with pain and had shit all over the seat and the floor, and you sat down with him and held him and whispered loving words, and took him back to his village where you eventually helped him to die. He would not have survived life on the village streets with two broken legs. You got a rabies shot yourself that day and got back on your moped and fed the dogs deep into the night.

On your way to the hospital, you made your friends stop three times. All of the medicine and various drugs you used on the dogs were tucked inside an oversized belt bag you wore like a rosary around your slim waist. Your first stop was for a dog who needed a rabies shot. The second was for a dog who needed another dose of homeopathic medicine. The third was for a dog with mange. You applied the oil with shaking hands as the sun began to fall behind the palms and banana trees, and finally—after that last one—you sat down against the brown leather seats laced with memories and you fell asleep.

By the time you woke, your body was clean, you wore a blue hospital gown instead of your usual dusty clothes, and everything around you was white and silver. There were no puppies curled up along dirt roads, shining orange in the sunlight. There were no Tamil men demanding that you help their cows or their goats. Only your friends beside you, holding your hands, wishing you well, but you were dying and they knew it and you knew it and there was nothing you could do anymore.

So you just felt love for the doctors who were trying to help you to the people who visited bringing you flowers you barely noticed. You loved everyone, human and dog alike, again and it was like feeling love for the first time. *They all matter, don't they?* You thought to yourself. *Not just the dogs, but everyone.*

I watched you from the small windows near the ceilings. I made myself invisible and watched the people in the waiting room. The intensive care unit of this hospital was a place where the people in this part of South India had to pay for their treatment, and in return they got a fancy-looking hospital of cement buildings painted white and manicured grounds dotted with palm trees and bushes of fragrant jasmine flowers. Most people who made it here weren't exactly well enough to appreciate the scenery, though I supposed their families did. Not all of them of course. Grief was prevalent.

The rooms of the Intensive Care Unit were filled with beds, but the nurses and doctors catered to their patients all day and night. I wasn't scared for you here. I was happy that your friends and community found the money to pay for your care like this. The government hospital would have been merciless and overcrowded. Here, they only allowed visitors to ICU patients access to the patients two at a time. Which wasn't always ideal.

I watched the people waiting to visit loved ones who were dying. It was fascinating to me. Three young girls were waiting in line; ready to don the facemasks and smocks the hospital provided to keep everything sterile. They were wearing perfect pastel-colored punjabis and had long silky hair and make-up on their faces. They blended together in a rainbow of fabric: one yellow, one blue, and one pink. Each girl had jasmine in her hair and a small gold flower nose ring in her left nostril. They held hands. They were terrified. I felt their fear inside my own feathers, ruffling them up. When I looked into the kajal-coated eyes of one of them, I heard her thoughts. They were waiting to see their mother. Everyone in the room waited with them.

I was still in the window when they returned five minutes later. The waiting room went quiet as they passed through the doors. They moved in a dancer's union to the bottom of the stairs, sank down to the floor, and wailed. Their almost musical moans resounded throughout the room. Their volume rose and fell as if they were lonely birds caught screaming into a storm.

The image of those girls on the floor, their sobbing faces and shaking bodies, made me realize that perhaps inside my owl heart, I felt this way about you even though I had never spoken to you directly, and even though I had the power in my claws to change your existence. I could send you somewhere better than another life.

But would you be happy if I named you Nāya and made you a god of dogs? I didn't know for sure if you'd prefer to continue on in samsara and help the dogs from the body of another human.

Where could I send you? Where would you dream to go—if you could decide?

An older man ran to the three sisters in the waiting room. They drew him into their huddle. The man was their father. His wife had just died. I knew you heard the news as well because I moved to an interior window to watch the nurses cover the body and carry her away. I watched you then, too. You were worried for the daughters and the husband. You felt such pity. I understood that maybe humans don't fit into glasses after all, or maybe, their energies can be restored with rest and then their hearts can open wider. You loved people, too. I knew it for certain then. So should you be a god of dogs or not?

After a while, the haggard father, dressed smartly in Western pants and a buttoned-down shirt, ushered his daughters outside. They walked down a path between the palm trees until they were beside the perfectly shorn grass. There they collapsed in a heap of colors like a flower closing its petals.

I see beauty in the ways that you humans cry, the ways you love.

The new operation for your cancer didn't help. Your mother was far away, only accessible through a cell phone call. Your face lit up when you spoke to her. I felt Lakshmi calling me, so I had to leave you.

"How much longer must you remain apart from me?" She asked me when I returned.

"You know I am yours, Lakshmi. I will return when you tell me to return," I replied, but she knew my thoughts as easily as if she were inside my body of feathers.

"I wish for you to follow through with this human. How much longer will it take?"

"Weeks perhaps. I still haven't decided whether to make the human a god of dogs or not."

"Then make haste. Keep watch. Listen to your own voice and not the human's."

I might have asked her, "How did you know I was considering asking the human?" but I didn't have to. She was Lakshmi and her wisdom was greater than mine.

When I returned, you seemed to have aged years rather than days.

Your friends clamored around you when they could. They came and went. Some cried while others shook their heads. You didn't want anyone to worry. You kept the dogs in your heart until the very end.

I had to wait until you died. I couldn't get close to you without the doctors or the nurses seeing me.

You passed in the night, melting into the darkness the way I have done so many times when I've carried souls to their next lives. As your soul escaped its body, it glowed in the same hue of orange as the dogs curled up along the dirt streets.

I took your shining soul into my feathery embrace, and I guided you to another human body.

<u>For My Mother</u>

<u>I stole you</u> from the mountain.

You sat with your eyes closed and your back against the stone. I crept up along the ledge of granite, stepping carefully with my paws.

"A wolf!" You exclaimed with your hands instead of your voice.

I looked into your eyes, and with a slight tilt of my head, I shifted out of my wolf-skin to reveal my other body: a human with long, tangled gray and black hair, blue eyes like yours but lighter, feet and hands full of scars from the long journeys I take each year across these mountains.

As you stood in surprise, you almost fell down into the pine trees on the lower trail. I promise I would have caught you. I hadn't eaten in weeks. It was almost winter and the leaves that were red as blood, yellow as fire, orange as the glow I get inside my eyes when I'm hungry.

I approached you cautiously. Last year I lost my kill and almost starved. I didn't want to make the same mistake again. Every year, it's harder.

"You're a wolf," you signed again. "And a girl? What are you?"

I almost feel pity when the human has no fear, when they don't realize their life will be over in minutes.

I gave you more than minutes, though. I gave you hours. Long enough for the sun to set over the horizon of trees around us. Long enough for us to tell each other a story. Like a mirror of a mirror, we reflected each other's sorrow. Our loss.

Our mothers.

I wasn't sure I believed in anything after death, but that day, I almost felt my mother's breath on the back of my neck.

She was a brave, strong wolf. Her fur was auburn. I got my father's markings and color—gray. But my mother moved through the forest like a small fire burning ahead of me, just out of reach. I could never touch her as much as I wanted to touch her. I could never be near her enough, close enough to whatever was inside her skin making her move.

Most days, she scanned the horizon, listening for news from other shifters, other wolves who weren't just wolves. We were a dying breed. Human killed real wolves, our distant kin, in such large numbers that it hurt us, too. Now, there's an unseen war going on between those of us that remain and humans. Your kind shouldn't have done what they did. They're bloodthirsty fools. Always wanting more. *Nothing is ever enough for you, is it?*

I knew it wasn't you personally that killed my mother, but every small human death is a comfort to the great death of my mother: the wolf fae who heard everything.

I don't mean she just heard news of our kind. No—you see—my mother could speak to crows, too. And bluebirds.

Swallows. Hawks.

No one in our pack could understand it.

My mother would shift into a woman with long auburn hair that covered her back and chest in waves like a cape. She was naked, but she kept herself hidden inside the mane of her hair like something even more mystical than us. Then, she would *crow*, or *caw*, or *hoo*, or make some kind of whirling sound none of us could comprehend.

I felt more sympathetic to your undecipherable sign language because of my mother's undecipherable bird language. I listened to you in a way I had never listened to a human before. I didn't need to know your language of hands because I could hear your thoughts. I don't hear every animal's thoughts, but humans think so loud, you don't even need to open your mouths or move your hands for me to hear you.

Your story was different than mine.

Your mother was sick. You only knew her from the side of a hospital bed. Her weak hand in your own grew smaller and smaller as your hand grew larger until she was little more than bones. Until her heart stopped.

"She was happy to die," you told me. "Her life was full of pain. If only she didn't have me. If only she didn't push herself that hard to bring another stupid person into the world. She could've done something with her life."

You grabbed one beer after another out of your bag. In the course of our few hours together, you drank seven. I thought beer tasted like piss and told you with gestures. You laughed and drank more. Drinking until you fell off the mountain would've been your punishment.

I saved you from that. That's what I tell myself when I think of what happened after our stories ended.

My story's ending:

My mother stood under the hemlocks. She raised her head, listening to the birds. She looked at me. Her eyes were auburn fires, glowing in the sunset, just like the glow of blue in your eyes reflecting the sky. I saw my mother overlapping you as I explained; "The bullet entered her chest right over her heart. I never saw where it came from."

You cried for me, for my mother.

It gave me pause, but it wasn't the same incapacitating pause as my mother's when she was shot by the hunter, nor the same as yours when you saw me shift and then stayed to chat. I saw my mother in the lines of your face, the creases the sun made, the pink tip of your nose. Memory holds power over me.

I leaped onto you deftly.

By the time my teeth found your neck, I was a wolf again. A wolf who'd lost her mother years ago. Who then lost her pack. A wolf alone is no creature to be reckoned with. Nor a woman, right? I would bite you no matter what story you told me—*for my mother*.

I ate you slowly, leaving only your backpack, your clothes, and your beer cans.

Someone would find you. Humans always found that trail when there were no clouds to obstruct their view.

Some will live. Some will die. Maybe I'll talk to them first, but I'll still eat them.

You all have different faces. Some of you are kind, some

cruel, some filled with so much joy, I feel joy again, too. But the truth remains: you killed my mother and it cost much more than any of you can pay. I will steal you. I will eat you until I'm not hungry anymore. Until my mother is avenged. Until I can walk through a forest without seeing any of your kind again.

Huldra

<u>I stole you</u> from the cave at the foot of the brown cliffs where the birds fly in wide circles and the trolls once lived long ago.

That cave was where many of them turned to stone, making the cliffs rise higher and higher. People died up there sometimes. They climb too far, as if they're reaching for something no one else has found. Was that why you walked miles away from the nearest town to that particular cave?

I watched you sit cross-legged in meditation.

You observed the distant flight of the gyrfalcons for a long time before you closed your eyes. I moved closer until I froze myself into the shape of a rock so I could watch you from inches away, smelling the sweat you hid beneath the musky scents you layered over yourself. Why do humans hide their scent? Don't they realize it's the most blatant of self-betrayals?

I wondered whether you'd be respectful or not. I couldn't tell by the way you sat there so still for so long. So I waited with you. I was hungry, but I don't eat just anyone. I wait to discover the kind of human they are.

I'm used to waiting.

My name itself—Huldra—means "hidden." I hide and people bring me offerings.

I hide and sometimes people anger me, so I take them. I step out of the stone or a cave and I show them how beautiful I am—the curves of my body, my perfect face, the curls of my long hair.

I don't show them my tail. I don't let them see that I am part serpent. I'm the kind of creature humans haven't seen in so many years, they've forgotten we exist. Humans are so egotistical that they believe they have created us when really—we were here first. We are as old as the pine trees or the dirt. We've always been here and we will be here long after your kind has gone. I won't be surprised if you are destroyed within the next century. You are careless. You don't respect the Earth anymore.

Finally you opened your eyes.

Your cell phone was vibrating against your chest. When you pulled it out, I expected you to put it to your ear the way other humans usually did. But you didn't. You held it in front of you and began moving your hands in front of your body. Were you speaking with your body to someone else inside the phone? Technology was something I hated. I had lived for so long in the mountains. I didn't usually have to see it so close to my home. But the way you were talking without your voice was curious. I wanted to know more about your language of hands. I thought you might be someone I didn't have to steal.

When your phone conversation was finished, you stood and turned toward the cave. You walked into it to examine the wet rock, the trickle of water running down the left side of the entrance, the chain other humans had lodged into the stone so they could climb up to a passageway that led miles into the Earth, under the rocks and the mountains. Humans usually didn't go there very often.

I stepped up behind you.

You jumped when you turned and saw me standing so close. I wondered what life was like for you if you couldn't hear things like footsteps or people's voices.

I waved instead of speaking.

"I'm deaf," you said with your voice, which sounded different than other people's voices. It was like you had a foreign accent. I imagined that was because you couldn't hear yourself.

I nodded and smiled, careful not to turn my body around because you might see the tail peeking out from the back of my skirt. If you saw me—I wouldn't have a choice.

"Have you been up there?" you asked me, pointing to the passageway at the top of the chain.

I shook my head and mimed a human climbing a chain only to slip down and die. I didn't want you to do anything stupid before I decided what to do with you.

You shrugged your shoulders and said, "I like to climb! I'm very careful, but if you're nervous, you can stick around to make sure I'm okay."

I wanted to stop you, but I don't meddle in the lives of humans unless they anger me.

You made the climb easily enough, turned and shouted down, "That was easy!"

Then you turned around and disappeared down the passage.

I waited again.

I didn't feel dread. I didn't worry. I just watched the gyrfalcons circling the cliffs until it was too dark to see them clearly anymore, and the mouth of the cave was as dark as pitch. I loved those birds. They were gorgeous birds of prey, always searching the mountains for ptarmigans or rodents sneaking between the rocks below. I understood birds of prey because if I were a bird, they were the kind that I would be. I lived too long taking humans to be less than that.

I wondered if you had a flashlight. I wondered if you were prepared for the cave to go on and on the way it did before the small opening on the other side—too small in fact, for any human to slip through. That was how very few people died, because not many people would walk so far into that cave without eventually turning around. Hardly anyone trusted that there might be an opening on the other side, fifteen kilometers down through the darkness. You seemed smarter than that. I didn't think you'd make it that far at all. I figured you'd be back soon. Any moment now.

I curled up and turned to stone to sleep.

The next morning was gray. The gyrfalcons circled around through the low clouds, blending in even when the clouds were behind them. They had the look of ghosts; mere outlines of the powerful birds they once were rather than the birds themselves.

You had not returned. At least you hadn't died from

falling down along the chain. That would have been messy and I didn't want to get your blood all over my new dress.

I waited for another day and another.

Two weeks passed, and I knew that by then you had died.

I climbed the cave wall up to the passage because I could do it effortlessly. I walked through the darkness for nearly two kilometers before I found your body curled up against the flowstone and stalagmites, cold and blue-skinned.

Why didn't you come back to the mouth of the cave?

What were you doing that far down? Was it suicide? Or just mindless curiosity? An overreaching sense of adventure?

I listened to the soothing sounds of dripping water from the stalactites above me, wondering for a brief moment what it was like to walk through a cave without being able to hear.

I picked you up and carried you on my back to the entrance and down the chain to where the gyrfalcons still circled round and round above my head and the moss and bush-covered hills looked like waves of green all the way down to the valley below and the distant village and beyond that—a lake glittered in the sunlight.

Deaf or hearing. Blind or seeing. Disabled or not—all you humans are the same, aren't you? You're always leaping too high for your bodies to land without breaking. You're always assuming you can do anything.

Well, you can't. You're not invincible. You're not gods or fae.

If only you were able to listen to the voice that speaks

from deep inside yourselves. Because that voice comes from the dirt, from stone and caves, because we all come from that if you go back far enough.

No life exists in utter solitude.

No creatures exist alone.

I carried your body to my own cave, way up on the side of the cliffs by the gyrfalcon nests. I fed until I was full and turned back into stone to sleep.

<u>So Many of You Want to Die</u>

<u>I stole you</u> because you wanted to die.

It was never about me. Who I am—or what I am—doesn't matter. You flirted with death in so many ways before you even noticed that I was watching you. Before you realized someone was noticing that you were not having an easy time being alive. So many humans live with so much guilt, so much blackness.

I'm tired. I'm tired because I've lived for hundreds of years and only the souls of suicides sustain me. I shouldn't exist.

I. Should. Not. Exist.

There is it, though. Another gunshot. Another head in a bag. Another body dangling from the ceiling. Another wrist slashed. Another person falling down from a bridge, off a cliff, down a waterfall. You're so creative as a species, and it shows in the ways you decide to die.

You had a thing for rivers. You wrote poems about them while sitting in your canoe. We spent weeks floating on the lake while you wrote in a leather-bound journal and promptly tore each page out and placed it in the water.

✿

Let me go back.

I came to you when you tried to die in the woods. You brought cases of beer and sleeping pills. There were days where I was busy with other suicides, so I didn't see you camping by the lake, writing by day and swimming naked each night by the light of the moon.

On what was supposed to be your last night, you took down your tent, packed your truck, took the pills, and walked back into the woods to the shore of the water.

I can take any form, but I like wolves best. Their fur is warm and soothing to me against the chill of the air in the evenings. I sat within the shadow of the hemlock trees just close enough to watch you drinking beer after beer. You crushed each can meticulously and placed them in a recycling bag. You cared about nature in a way that other suicides didn't. If only some other fae could have stolen you. If only you were transformed into something else so you wouldn't want to die. So many humans are not human deep down—they're something else trapped in human bodies, stuck in their towns and cities, confined by their jobs.

I wished I could set them free.

I wished I could set you free.

The pills began to take effect quickly as you drank.

On your third beer, your hand slipped and you slumped down on the sand. A poem you were writing fell out of your hands.

I moved closer, but the wind stole the paper before I could read it. I heard something in the trees and moved back in the shadows.

A friend of yours rushed over to your sleeping form. I knew it was a friend because she kissed your cheeks, she tried mouth-to-mouth, and when that didn't work, she took you over her shoulder and carried you away.

I waited.

I found other suicides and consumed them.

Months later you returned to the same spot—alive.

This time I couldn't stay hidden. I took human form, a plain brown-haired, brown-eyed girl.

I walked up to you and sat down.

"Hey," you said. "You want a beer?"

"Okay," I replied with my voice, but I also signed. A deaf person had just killed himself by leaping off a cliff in the mountains not far from us. When I take people, I take their memories, their bodies, their language. The signing enamored me. I was so excited I could finally try it out on you, even if you didn't understand it.

"Are you deaf?" you said while handing me a can.

"No, I just finished some classes in sign language and I like using it," I said while signing at the same time. It wasn't something deaf people did very often because it dilutes their language, but I wanted to sign so badly and if I only used my hands, you'd never have understood me.

"It's cool. I like watching your hands. I write poems. Maybe you could tell me a story in sign and I could try writing it down and see how close I get to the real meaning? Do you know enough sign to try that?"

You had no way of knowing how many poets I had taken.

You had no way of knowing how much I've loved them all—loved poets more than any of my human casualties.

They're like shiny coins at the bottom of a fountain, made beautiful by the waters they use to drown themselves, the ways that they drift toward death. Sylvia Plath was one of the greatest poets who ever lived. I was certain of it. I replayed her death so many times in my head after it happened because it was the only time I was completely at one with her. She and I shared her body for those precious moments of her departure while her children slept fitfully in the other room. The thoughts that ran through her head were enough to sustain me for years. I lived and breathed her words. I played them back again and again like music. If I could have helped anyone to live forever, never to stop writing poems, it would have been Sylvia.

I knew you would succeed in dying eventually, too. All of you did. But for a little while, I fancied the thought that if I could hold you in my arms, I could read the soul you inked into the page not after you died but before it. I had taken so many, but I rarely knew them *before*.

I smiled, took a sip of beer, and began:

"I don't remember how I was born exactly. My first memory is blood flooding a bath from the wrists of a human girl. My second memory is the inside of an oven, warm air, sleep. My third memory is the taste of gasoline, filling me, thickening in my throat. My fourth memory is so much water, flooding my lungs, suffocating me, the thick liquid air pushing me down, down, down. I didn't cry at first. Not for years.

"But lately, the fact that I am made of humans who choose to die, who self-destruct, weighs me down. I feel myself wanting to die too, but every time one of you kills yourself, I become stronger. I couldn't always take physical form, but now I can take nearly any form. Now I can be a wolf every night if I wish it. I can roam the woods and the cities. But every time a person takes their life, my soul is sucked into their body and I feel everything they feel, I die with them, only to wake up stronger for the next. I die every day. And now, for just a little while, I am hoping you don't kill yourself too soon. I am hoping for a reprieve. A break from so much death. Time to float instead of drown. Please?"

I felt the tears in my eyes mirroring the tears on your cheeks. I knew you couldn't have understood me, but maybe, somewhere inside of you—you did understand?

You put down your pen because your hand was shaking. "I—" you started, took a sip of beer, and continued, "—I don't know what to say."

"Did you write a lot?" I asked, peering down at the messy handwriting in your journal but you closed it before I could read anything.

"No. I think—I think I felt your story more than I could make sense of anything you said and it hurt my heart. I don't know if—do you need to tell me with your voice? Like—somehow it seemed you were saying things you don't really want me to know …"

I smiled at your kindness. I wanted to voice it then—to tell you the whole bloody truth of my existence.

But I couldn't.

Something stopped me, maybe the same thing that made you close your journal and never show me the words you wrote—the lines you pulled out of the air between my hand shapes and movements.

We weren't ready.

When you saw that I wasn't going to say or sign anything more, you took my hand and said, "What's your name?"

I was stumped. I didn't have a name. "Ummm …"

"You must have a name."

"Sylvia," I said finally, taking the name of my favorite suicide because in a small way, you reminded me of her.

"Okay. Well, I'm Sam. Do you like canoeing?"

"I've never been …" I said and signed.

Because I hadn't. I had only taken people from beneath the canoes, the ones who had flipped their own boats in order to drown in rapidly moving rivers. I wasn't sure if I should pretend I wasn't scared of that death—the slipping under the foam, the banging against the hard rocks below, the taste of blood in my mouth—or reveal it to you as an irrational fear.

"Do you want to go with me?"

I nodded while making the sign for "yes." Because I knew my fears were silly. You wouldn't die that way. That much I knew from our brief time together, from the way you spoke, the way you moved, the way you asked me to go canoeing.

I hoped that maybe my presence—as someone you didn't know closely, someone you imagined didn't even know you wanted to die—had the potential to help you discover a reason to live. I felt absurd. If people stopped killing themselves, I would die, too. I would disappear, wouldn't I? But that was exactly what I wanted, wasn't it? A reason to die for good.

I laughed as I followed you to the place where you tied

up your canoe along the shore. I was a suicidal suicide fae. *How ridiculous was that?*

Your canoe was red and beautiful. I don't know what I expected, but sitting at the bow facing the stern, facing you with a paddle in your hands and a case of beer at your feet next to a lifejacket, I felt at peace in a way I had never felt before. I smiled.

"You don't have to paddle if you don't want to," you said.

How did you know that all I wanted was to sit and watch you paddle while surveying the beaches we passed and the places where the trees grew all the way into the water, as if they didn't realize the water would spread and rise up their trunks? Those trees that stood waist-deep looked so much happier than the ones on land. Would they die sooner that way? I didn't know. There was so much I didn't know about the world, even though I had been alive for so long.

"What are you thinking about?" you asked me.

"The trees. The ones in the water," I spoke and signed and then pointed to them.

"Trees?" You used one hand but you signed the word back to me with a smile.

"Yes, that's it. That one's nice, huh?"

"Yeah. It's really intuitive. I like sign language. I wish I had time to—"

You stopped short, not realizing that I knew what the rest of your sentence was anyhow, oblivious to the fact that I would feel you then, I would feel everything you've ever done in your life as you died.

You looked at the trees and in that gaze I knew you

didn't entirely *want* to die. You loved the Earth, you loved trees and canoes and lakes. You loved to drink beer on the water and paddle around for hours, dreaming up poems in your head.

"Is it okay if we stop and float for a while?" you asked.

"Of course," I said and signed.

I wished I had a pen and paper then. I felt awkward just watching you take your journal out and start writing feverously. You wrote for five minutes and then you read what you wrote, ripped the page out of the journal, and dropped it into the water. You turned your poems into lily pads floating together in clusters. I saw a word here and there but I couldn't read them. The water dissolved your lines too quickly. I realized how fast you'd dissolve as a person.

I looked around. You paddled us to a hidden cove at the northernmost point of the lake. There were no other boats around. Only water slapping lightly against the pine and maple trees leaning over it. I crawled to the middle of the canoe.

"What are you doing?" you asked.

"I don't know. I'm not used to boats. Is it okay to be in the middle?" I spoke and signed.

You tilted your head to the side in consideration. I wasn't sure if I was being clear enough. I wanted you to love me, but I knew humans were not really able to control that emotion. I knew I'd likely fail. I should have chosen a prettier body. A nicer face.

"It's easy to flip the boat over," you eventually said, "I can paddle us over to that island, and we could tie off to that tree."

"Sure," I said.

"You don't have to move back to the end," you said and moved your left foot forward so that it rested against the side of my right calf. You knew what I was thinking. I was sure of it then. I felt such a gorgeous current of electricity between us, even though we weren't touching skin to skin.

"I wasn't going to," I signed, forgetting to use my voice.

You laughed. "I think I understood that one!"

I smiled back as the end of the canoe hit against the roots of the pine tree behind you that were sticking up out of the dirt. That tree looked as if it was trying to take a step forward into the water, trying to move instead of staying in one place for a hundred years. I understood it. I wanted to move, too. I wanted something more than death after death.

"So do you want to stay in the boat—or look around the island?" you asked.

"The boat," I signed, knowing you'd understand me because of how much the sign for "boat" looked like a boat itself.

"Okay. Do you want another beer?"

"Not yet," I said instead of signing, while staring at you with so much hunger in my eyes I must have looked desperate.

"Okay," you said.

You kneeled in the boat and moved toward me until we were both kneeling face to face. The boat rocked, but with one end against the shore, it didn't threaten to topple us into the water. You took my face in your hands. You leaned in.

"Is this what you want?" you asked me softly.

I kissed you in response.

I wasn't sure how to do it. I had never kissed someone before. Your lips tasted faintly of cigarettes and beer. You seemed to know what you were doing with your tongue, so I kept my lips slack and let you kiss me back so beautifully I felt you like a shimmer over my skin, from my mouth down my neck, down my chest, down my legs, all the way to my toes. My whole body hummed.

You pressed your body against mine so tightly, I fantasized that we were already one person—our clothes were just more skin, that's all. You peeled off your shirt slowly while kissing me, but when I moved to pull my own shirt off, you stopped my hands. You shook your head. You lifted your hand up inside my shirt to my belly. You stroked me there and the tremor it caused below your hands was so intense I had to grasp the sides of the boat to steady myself.

Humans did this all the time?!

Why had I never thought to try it?!

I was losing sense of myself, of you, of the boat and the water, of the world. I felt free for the first time. I wasn't reliving someone's life, I was living a life of my own, however briefly, and finally—I was making love like a person—I was making love with a person.

We lay down in the bottom of the boat and you did things I had only seen through windows, through your movies and poetry. I never realized what ecstasy could feel like. It wasn't like suicide at all.

Death was the greatest farce of human lives. It didn't make

anyone feel free. It wasn't a release. It was an abrupt end. A painful moment that, once begun, always ended in a flash of nothingness.

Love—or whatever we did in that canoe—was freeing.

Once I knew that, I wasn't sure how I could go back. How to take suicide after suicide. How to feel any sort of fulfillment from death again.

We lay in the boat until the sky grew dark.

I may have fallen asleep against your arm.

Time didn't seem to exist until … under the darkness of a black moon, you stroked my hair. I didn't want to speak. I wanted you think I was fast asleep and couldn't be woken. I was scared of what it would mean to move again, to sit up in the canoe and have to paddle back to wherever it was you came from.

Sex was just a way to forget, wasn't it? It was an expression of love when it was done right, the way I think we did it, but ultimately it gave humans a momentary sense of euphoria. No suicide wanted to die during an orgasm. No human would choose death before one more chance to have sex. But how much could we do it before you'd eventually remember that you really did want to die and that desire wasn't going to just magically disappear? Sex was so much better than death, but it couldn't replace it.

Before I could stop myself, I began to cry.

"Are you okay? What happened? What's wrong?"

Your empathy was so deep, I felt you asking me from inside of myself instead of outside. *Was that because we just had sex? Or was it something about you as a person?*

I decided some version of the truth was in order. I signed and spoke, "I was here when you took those pills. I've been wandering in the woods for a while now."

"But that was months ago! Have you stayed out here that long? Do you have a campsite somewhere?"

"I left and came back and I happened to see you today. It was an accident. I've been away from here, too."

"That's so weird. And sad. I mean—I'm sorry if I scared you or—what did I do exactly? Why are you with me right now?"

"I saw you and I wanted to help but I didn't know how."

"Wait—is that why you wanted to do this?"

The question hurt because it was both true and untrue at the same time and I didn't know how to say that. "No—I mean—not the only reason. I didn't plan this. It just sort of happened. Really, I didn't seduce you to try and make you want to live again."

But as the words tumbled out of my mouth, into my hands, and you both heard and saw them, I knew—and you knew—it was one of the truest things I had ever said.

You buried your face in my shoulder and you cried.

I cried with you. I stroked your hair. I looked up at the stars without knowing what the fuck I could possibly do to fix you, to fix me, to give us that happy ending so many of your movies and novels aspire to give their characters.

"Let's just run away? Please? I don't know you that well, but I really like you. Maybe I love you. Maybe this is something that could help us both want to live again," I whispered.

You kept your face buried in my chest, against the beat

of my heart. Your arms held me tightly around my waist, as if you were afraid of slipping away, too.

I looked up at the stars. I prayed. I didn't know much about the world aside from how people chose to die. But I wanted to know more. I wanted you to show me.

After a while, you sat up.

Your eyes were red-rimmed, and you grabbed another beer and took a long sip before you said, "Okay. I don't always want to die, you know. I love these trees. I love this boat. I love the water. I love the air. I love people. I love the sky and the stars. And I probably love you, too, even though I don't know you very well. I don't understand why I get so depressed. I wish I could shut it off or lock it out. Sometimes I call it a black dog, this—sadness that threatens to rip me apart, that makes me just want to stop and … end everything."

You drank the rest of the beer, lit up a joint, and smoked in silence.

You offered me the joint and I took it. I had never smoked anything before, but I was human, wasn't I? *I should try everything.*

The smoke tasted sweet, but I coughed hard after only one hit.

You patted me on the back until I stopped coughing. I looked around. The trees were dancing, the stars shone brighter, and the water played a song against the side of the canoe.

There was so much to live for wasn't there? So much that you humans throw away when you decide to die. I didn't understand it, but at the same time, *I did* because I had felt hundreds of suicides happen inside my own body. I felt their needs rising like incoming tides—or like giant black dogs made of darkness—surpassing everything else, washing the world away or tearing it apart.

You were looking at me when I stopped staring at the water and the sky. You eyes were round with hope. I didn't know how much longer you had, but I wanted to watch you, too. I wanted to learn about your world, about our world, before both of us died.

"Let's just keep floating," you said. "There's another island over that way."

Seed

I stole you from the snow.

The wind blew hard for many days. I moved slowly over the white land, squinting from the brightness of the ground. It looked as if all the stars from the sky fell down and covered the Earth. It felt strange for me to even think that name— Earth. There were no jungles or deserts anymore; only a great arctic land, only snow.

I sometimes liked to scream or sing very loud because I knew no one would hear me.

I was alone.

For days that became weeks that became months, I never saw any sign of life. No animals. No humans. Even the trees had fallen, covered in the white star blankets.

I almost didn't see the waving tuft of black hair, the layers of cloth covering your body, the stick you held in your small hand. I put my hands against your skin as if to confirm the truth I already knew—you were frozen. You had been this way for years perhaps, but once upon a time, you breathed, you laughed, you held this small stick in your hands, you ran.

It took me hours to pry you from the ice. Even when

I pulled too hard and one of your tiny dark fingers was left behind in the snow, your blood didn't run. I lifted your skeletal body in my arms, shaking from the cold, but resolved. I would do it—I would carry you as far as I could.

Each step I took was harder at first, but, like most journeys, I fell into a sort of awkward shuffle, a rhythm of me taking step after step with the weight of you cradled in my arms and then on my hip. I finally balanced you across my shoulders with my head bent down and I kept going.

I walked throughout the too-bright day until everything was dark except for the white land. Walking at night made me feel as if I were walking across the face of the Moon. Everything was made of crystalline, sharp edges. The world had gone cold. It lost its fire long, long ago.

I had never seen a human before.

I am called a ghost, you see. Or a fae thing. I am both, I think—ghost and faery. But that also means I am—I mean, I suppose I was—human.

I was just like you—the frozen child.

I was human, too, but I am too old now. I've lived too long in this ghost form that I don't remember my old life. I don't remember you, child. Even your body, the way you had to move, the clothes you had to wear, the things you did, your passions. I wish I knew you better. I only carry snippets of a time long past—shards of sound. Music was the easiest thing for me to remember, and even that has now faltered.

I looked at your face hanging from my shoulder as I walked.

Your white eyes so close to mine, urged me to stretch my thoughts back as far as I could—and when I went there, when I reached for the farthest piece—I heard a song in my head:

For he comes, the human child
To the waters and the wild,
With a faery hand in hand
For the world's more full of weeping
Than you can understand …

Thus I sang to you.

I sang the song with the words "frozen child" instead.

I only remembered the chorus, those five lines, but somehow inside them, I felt a deep understanding of everything, the entire world that humans made and the fae who came with it—because you know, child—that we all have come from you. You made us, not the other way around. You gave us life and reason, and we only took from you what you decided we should take.

Don't you see?

You made your own world because your dreams are your lens, your way of seeing, which means they decide your world.

I wanted to know why you held that stick.

I wanted to know where your clothes came from, what tribe was your family, what culture you came from, and what you believed was happening around you.

I wanted to know your gods, the things you loved beyond all measure, the things you used to measure all things against. Were they people? Were they animals? Or had the animals all died out by the time you were alive?

I wasn't sure. The animals went first, but I don't know how soon humans followed. I only knew the great white shining space you left behind.

The planet you left behind to freeze.

I hated all humans a little bit.

They destroyed themselves. As a species, they were suicidal.

But I had never seen a child frozen in the snow. I had never known compassion before I found it in your eyes, in the trapped motion of your arms, the stick in your hands, your curled legs. Your body told me a sad story I couldn't let lie. I couldn't leave you there in the snow to stay frozen. I didn't know if my carrying you would do anything at all. I only knew that I couldn't do anything else. I needed you. I was alone before I found you.

I carried you for days.

Sometimes I sat down in the snow to rest with your head in my lap.

I stroked your black hair until it wasn't frozen anymore and I could feel its tight curls in my fingers. I imagined I was wind and I let your hair move through my fingers because I was a ghost and I could make myself less than corporal when I wanted. I could actually *be air*. Though most of the time I chose not to, preferring a solid body so that I could take one step after another through the snow, so that I could feel more like a part of the world.

I didn't want to be a ghost.

❧

Sometimes I laid you down in the snow and then laid myself over you, melting into the form of your body. You were emptied of soul, of feeling, of anything you had before. I couldn't learn about your past, I couldn't feel anything but the frozen blood and organs, the rags tucked around your skin, and that stick in your hands.

In my dreaming, I saw you as a strong child with your face against the wind and your hair blowing behind you like a dark cape. I saw the stick as your weapon, your talisman. You swung it over your head. You made battle cries to an empty plain surrounded in jagged peaks. You ruled the white lands. Everything covered in snow was yours. You dug holes in search of frozen animal bodies for food. Your stick guided you, helping you to find just the right places to dig so that you wouldn't lose precious energy by digging ten holes before you found something to eat.

You fed on iced meat by the light of the moon washing over the land. You ate the snow for water, holding clumps of it in your mouth until they melted.

For many years, you were alone, growing from a small child to a teenager. Sometimes you liked to dance with your stick. You spun it round your head, you threw it, you leaped over it, you held it like a dance partner, wishing for someone. You lay down in the snow and wished and wished until one day you sat up and saw the silhouette of another creature on the horizon.

You ran so fast, you couldn't even feel your legs and you almost left your stick behind.

The other human was so cold you gave her your extra animal skins. You embraced each other full of the knowledge that you were both alone, so there was no reason to be particular. You could love each other like the last people on Earth.

Days became years.

You grew old together.

When your partner couldn't dig for their food anymore, you did it for her.

When she couldn't walk anymore, you carried her on your back and used your stick to help you bear the extra weight.

When all she could do was lie down in the snow, you lay down with her.

I dreamed that you two died hand in hand so that neither of you would be alone. Your hearts stopped beating one and then the other like a song.

When I opened my own eyes, I looked down at your unfrozen black hair on your still-frozen body. I lifted you again and walked until I was at the foot of the mountains. For the first time in my existence, I began to climb.

I don't know how many days or weeks I spent climbing.

Walking uphill felt the same as walking across the valleys. There was nothing but snow and sky and rock around me. I kept going until I reached a small plateau with a view for kilometers all around me. I felt like I could see the entire world of snow spread out before me.

I had to do something besides dream.

I had to dig.

I took the stick out of your hands in order to dig my own hole in the snow. I had gotten used to walking across this land but I wasn't used to doing something like that. I had to focus every ounce of my energy on the task of making a child-shaped hole for you to rest, though it wasn't really for you to be buried.

I needed to plant you.

I dreamed that if I laid you down inside the snow and covered your frozen limbs, that maybe—if I planted enough hope with your body, if I spent every day from then onwards sitting beside you—maybe you would grow.

Perhaps I wasn't left alone, the last creature on a frozen planet, burying a dead child. Perhaps through your burial you could become something else.

So I laid you down. I laid you down carefully inside the hole and covered you in the white dust.

I dreamed you could be a seed.

Acknowledgments

The story "A Murder of Two" previously appeared in *Callisto: A Queer Fiction Journal*.

This book couldn't have happened without my retreat time spent at Gullkistan Residency for Creative People in Iceland nor my time in Amsterdam, Thailand, and India. These stories were born out of my experiences with the elves in Iceland in particular, which opened me to all the other fae I've connected with thus far. I'm thankful for the Fuseli painting *The Nightmare*, which partially inspired my story "The Dream Thief." I'm grateful to everyone I've spoken with about fae creatures and everyone who has read some of these stories. You are all magical to me and far too many to name.

Some of the stories are dedicated to the following people:
"The Dream Thief" is for Jaimee.
"Shining Orange" is for Ann.
"So Many of You Want to Die" is for Sean, Sylvia, Anne, Virginia, and the rest of them.

About the Author

Kristen Ringman is a deaf writer, traveler, and mother. She writes multi-cultural lyrical fiction and poetry inspired by her persistent wanderings to far off places. She is the author of *Makara: a novel* (Handtype Press), a Lambda Literary finalist in Debut Fiction, and the editor of *Everyday Haiku: an anthology* (Wandering Muse Press). She received her MFA from Goddard College in 2008. She's currently working on her first poetry collection and literary fiction novels that play with the boundaries of magical realism, fantasy, and horror. Her work can be found in various anthologies such as *Deaf Lit Extravaganza* and *QDA: A Queer Disability Anthology*. [kristenringman.com]